A VERY *Perry* CHRISTMAS

MARIE LANDRY

Copyright 2020 Marie Landry

All rights reserved

No part of this book may be reproduced in any form or by any electronic or mechanical means, including information storage and retrieval systems, without written permission from the author, except for the use of brief quotations in a book review.

This book is a work of fiction. Names, characters, places, and incidents are the product of the author's imagination or are used fictitiously. Any resemblance to any actual places, events, or people, either living or dead, is coincidental.

Cover illustration by Nadezda Vinogradova
Cover designed by Marie Landry

ALSO BY MARIE LANDRY

Blue Sky Days
The Most Wonderful Time of the Year
Waiting for the Storm (Angel Island #1)
After the Storm (Angel Island #2)
Take Them by Storm (Angel Island #3)
Mistletoe Kiss
Only You
Maybe You
Hung Up on You

To everyone who still believes in the magic of Christmas, even when life feels anything *but* magical.

And to Mum. Always.

CHAPTER ONE

"Are you sure about this? It's not too late to change your mind."

My boyfriend, Evan, paces around our bedroom as I stuff my toiletry bag into my suitcase. He pauses just long enough for me to give him a *we've-been-through-this* look.

He resumes his pacing, one hand planted on his hip and the other raking through his hair. Over the last year I've learned this is his biggest stress tell. He doesn't do it often since he's mostly an easy-going guy. When he gets like this, I always want to freeze him in his tracks and snuggle him.

So that's exactly what I do. Abandoning my suitcase, I round the bed and insert myself in his path. He comes to an abrupt halt, narrowly avoiding colliding with me. His hand fists in his hair and then releases it, leaving the dark locks standing on end.

I suppress a smile. He's so freaking adorable. His face softens as I smooth his hair and lean in for a quick kiss.

"I mean it, Gwen," he says. "It's not too late. We could unpack and hide out here for the next week. Get ourselves a Christmas tree from that pop-up in the Loyola Plaza, turn off our phones, pretend we've adopted the ways of a nudist colony..." He bounces his eyebrows in the way that never fails to make me laugh. With his hands on my hips, he pulls me closer for another kiss.

I only let his tongue tangle with mine for a few seconds before gripping his shoulders and putting an arm's length of distance between us. "A-plus for effort, but your usual distraction tactics won't work, Evan Perry. We've been together for almost a year and I haven't met a single member of your family. It's time."

Guilt flits across his face. Making him feel bad isn't my intention, but I'm not entirely sure he's kidding about ditching our plans in favor of staying in Bellevue for the holidays. I know the fact I haven't met his family yet isn't personal; like many people, Evan has a complicated history with his siblings, and their get-togethers are usually limited to big events and Christmas.

But after a whirlwind romance that turned into a serious relationship approaching its first anniversary, I feel like I won't have the complete picture of the man I love until I meet his family. Spending almost a week with them over Christmas isn't necessarily ideal, but it's how they've done things since their parents died, and I refuse to be the reason Evan bails this year.

With a drawn-out groan, he drops his head on my shoulder. "They're just…a lot, Gwen. It's going to be a week of forced family togetherness, awkward conversations, arguing, and general chaos. I don't want you seeing me differently once you realize what kind of gene pool I come from."

I give him a playful shove until he straightens. "Stop. The only thing that's going to make me see you differently is if you keep whining and stalling."

He lets out an exaggerated gasp, clutching at his chest. "You wound me. I do not *whine*, Gwendolyn."

My lips twitch. He's the only person I've allowed to call me by my full name since my dad died. He says he loves the way it feels and sounds, and that it's unique, like me—how could I resist? "You're whining."

He huffs. "Fine, fine. You're right, I'm being a baby. Just don't say I didn't warn you."

Oh, he's warned me all right. When we made the arrangements to spend a week over Christmas with his four siblings and their partners, he went so far as to make me index cards about each of them so I'd be prepared. Actual *index cards*. I haven't even met the Perry siblings, but I know their ages, occupations, where they live, and the character traits that make them annoying, at least according to Evan

I glide my hands over his shoulders and lock them behind his neck. "I may not know what it's like to be part of a big, noisy, over-the-top family with a mountain of emotional baggage, but I *do* know I love you more than anyone else in the entire world. Try to focus on that and the fact I'll be with you every step of the way. If you're really, truly miserable after a few days, we'll make some excuse and head back to the city."

Closing his eyes, he rests his forehead briefly against mine. "I love you more than anything too, which is why I want our first Christmas together to be perfect. My family may be nutty, but they do the picture-perfect Christmas well, and I know you've always wanted to see what that's like."

Growing up with a single dad and no other family besides a grandmother who lived across the country and couldn't care less about us, I've never experienced the type of Christmases I saw every year on TV. It's not that I felt I was missing out exactly—my dad always took time off work around the holidays and made sure it was a special time for us—but I've always been curious what it would be like to be part of a big family holiday. Traditions, chaos, drama, and all.

"If it gets to be too much, we can always skip out on family time and do our own thing, right?"

Evan chuckles, ducking his head and shaking it back and forth slowly. "Oh, Gwen. Sweet, innocent Gwen. There *is* no skipping out on Perry family togetherness. It is *all* Perry family togetherness."

I slide my arms from his neck to hook them around his hips. "*Maybe* we'll just have to get creative." I give his ass a squeeze and laugh when he yelps. "After all, you've never brought anyone home to meet the family before, right? Different rules should apply for couples."

Evan pulls me forward, closing the minuscule space between us. He bumps his nose gently against mine, one of our many signs of affection. When he pulls back, my gaze drops to his lips, which curve in a knowing smile. "We always did make up our own rules." His husky voice sends shivers racing along my skin and a shot of desire straight to my core.

I'm transported back to the moment before our first kiss: his mouth hovering over mine like it is now, anticipation building until I was nearly breathless. I remember hoping that excitement would never go away. A year later, I'm certain I'll always feel this tingly, electric *want-you-need-you-gotta-have- you* feeling whenever I'm with Evan.

Our lips meet in a soft, sweet kiss. I angle my head and Evan takes my cue, parting my lips with his tongue. He tastes like minty toothpaste and the strawberry Pop Tart he had for breakfast. I know he wants to take this kiss further—the evidence of his arousal is growing and pressing against my stomach—but we need to get on the road. I keep the kisses light, unable to stop right away, before finally putting a bit of space between us.

"Don't forget you'll finally get to see Hadley after nearly a year apart," I say, picking up our conversation as if we hadn't enjoyed a brief, lusty interlude.

Evan groans again. "If you wanted to kill the mood, talking about my baby sister is a surefire way to do it."

I bite my lip to hold in my laughter. His gaze drops to my mouth, eyes darkening again, and I quickly press my lips together and back away. "No. We need to go. For real this time."

"Are you absolutely sure? We could go back to bed right now and leave later today. If you want to talk about a mood killer, just wait 'til Jasper breaks out the schedule or Lina starts talking about the characters in her book as if they're real people."

I return to the bed and zip my suitcase closed. He's still standing where I left him, so I beckon him closer, feeling almost bad about the hopeful glint in his eyes. When he reaches me, I grip his sweater and lean in close. "We're leaving. Now."

He kisses me and moves away, saying over his shoulder, "Guess I'd better get used to the erection rejection. Being in a house with my siblings will effectively kill the mood for the next week."

I laugh so hard I nearly fall on the bed.

"Oh, hey, so…" Evan's voice is high and overly casual, practically shaking with laughter. This is never a good sign.

We've just pulled into the driveway of the rental house where we'll be spending the next several days. I've barely had time to take in the rustic two-story house set on a large plot of land before my focus shifts to him to see what he's up to.

He reaches into the pocket of his jeans and produces several crumpled index cards. He looks way too pleased with himself, the jerk. "Look what I found on the bedside table. You must have forgotten them, so I scooped them up for you."

With a gasp, I snatch the cards from him and stuff them in my purse. "What if your siblings found these and read them? You're the worst."

He makes a little hum of disagreement. "I am, in fact, the *best*. Trust me, you'll thank me for this later. Forewarned is forearmed, as my dad always used to say. Maybe we should go over the highlights one more time before we go inside."

"No!" It takes everything in me not to burst out laughing again. It would only encourage him. "Believe me, the contents of these cards are burned in my brain, Evan. Now quit your stalling."

The air holds a bite that causes our breath to fog the minute we step out of the car. We're only about thirty minutes from Bellevue, but the temperature drop is noticeable, and a light layer of fresh snow dusts the front lawn of the house. Picture-perfect setting for a Christmas getaway: check.

I've been so busy staring at the house, I didn't notice Evan getting both our bags from the trunk. He shakes his head and kisses my cheek when I reach for mine. "Jasper may be a control freak, but he can sure pick beautiful places to rent, I'll give him that."

As if summoned by his name, the front door opens and Jasper appears. I've seen pictures of all the Perry siblings, so I know who's who by sight, along with the various tidbits Evan oh-so-helpfully provided. Jasper is wearing the exact type of outfit Evan said he would be: a thick wool sweater and pressed trousers. His short, perfectly-coiffed hair is the same shade of dark-brown as Evan's, although a few silvery threads have worked their way in near the temples. As we approach the house, I see that where Evan's eyes are on the greener side of hazel, Jasper's are a rich, chocolaty brown.

Evan's flash card description of Jasper flits through my mind: thirty-nine, single, works as a bank manager in Toronto. Moved back into the family home when he was just twenty-three to raise Evan and Hadley, ages sixteen and fifteen respectively, after their parents died in a train crash. Stuffy, pompous know-it-all who's always right and has an opinion about everything.

We're all the way up to the front door before Jasper's serious expression finally eases into a smile. It's small, but it transforms his whole face, making him less severe-looking and unapproachable. He reaches for my hand and envelopes it in his large, warm one. "So nice to finally meet you, Gwen."

"You too, Jasper. I've heard a lot about you."

Jasper's already-tiny smile falters as his gaze slides to his brother. "Yes, I'm sure. Evan. You're looking well." He reaches out both arms and I think he's going to hug Evan, but he takes the suitcases from him instead. "Come inside where it's nice and warm. It was snowing shortly before you arrived, so I started a fire."

We troop inside after Jasper and shed our outerwear in the front hall before moving toward the spacious living room. Excitement bubbles up inside me as I take in the enormous fireplace with two framed Perry family photos on the mantel and a basket of stockings on the floor. Overstuffed couches and chairs surround a huge wooden coffee table, and a bay window overlooks the back of the property, which is a wide open space that ends in a line of coniferous trees. Evan catches my eye, and I let out a delighted laugh.

"This is perfect." I turn to Jasper, who's watching me expectantly, and repeat the words.

"I'm glad you think so," he says. "Evan told me it's always been a dream of yours to have a country Christmas, so I thought this place would do nicely. It'll look even lovelier once it's all decorated."

I stop myself from bouncing on my toes in excitement. Jasper isn't what I was expecting at all. Evan made him sound so stuffy and overbearing. I'll admit he does hold himself a bit stiff and his speech patterns are more formal than I'm used to, but he's sweet and thoughtful. I curb the urge to hug him since I'm pretty sure it would end up being more awkward than it's worth.

Jasper tells us we should join the others in the kitchen while he takes our bags to our room. We offer to take them ourselves, but he insists and heads for the staircase at the far end of the living room. Evan catches my hand, linking our fingers as we approach the kitchen.

"I know what you're going to say," he says softly. "Jasper doesn't seem so bad. The thing is, he makes a good first impression because he's Mr. Manners. Wait 'til he breaks out the schedule and starts setting timers on his phone. I wonder if he'll have house rules this year."

"He hasn't needed to instate house rules since you and Hadley learned not to overindulge in the eggnog," says a man's voice as we round the corner into the kitchen. Malcolm is a slightly shorter, younger version of Jasper in much more casual clothes. Unlike Jasper, he hops up from the stool he was sitting on to give Evan a back-thumping hug. He turns to me next and holds out his arms. "I doubt you got a hug from Jasper, but most of the rest of us are huggers."

"Good because I'm a hugger too." I step into the circle of his arms and he gives me a much gentler hug than the one he gave his brother. "It's nice to meet you, Malcolm."

"You too. 'Bout time, eh? I was beginning to get a complex, thinking Ev was keeping you away from us on purpose." He pokes Evan in the chest and laughs when he makes a disgruntled sound. "This is my beautiful wife, Sherée." He turns to the woman who just stepped up next to him. Her figure-hugging red sweater dress and knee-high black boots make her look like a sexy, dark-skinned Mrs. Claus.

"Welcome to the Perry madness," she says, hugging me tightly. She even smells like Christmas: baked apples and cinnamon. I like her already.

"Don't scare her off, Sherée," comes a woman's voice from behind them.

"I'm sure Evan has already warned her about us," Malcolm says, stepping aside to let Hadley through.

My heart floods with warmth as I watch Hadley launch herself into Evan's arms. His eyes close as he embraces her tightly, lifting her right off the ground. She lets out a squeak and they both laugh, but don't release each other for another few moments.

"It's so good to see you." Evan's voice is choked with emotion. The sound of it makes my eyes sting. Hadley is the one he's always talked about most, and the one he was closest to growing up. He often jokes that the two of them were dropped off by the stork a year apart and that's why they're so different from the other three Perry siblings.

"I'm sorry it's been so long." Hadley looks him over from head to toe and then hugs him again, this time briefly. "Okay, enough of this sappy shit or I'll start crying." She spins toward me, her dark curls bouncing. Her eyes are the same shade of hazel as Evan's, and just as warm. "Gwen. Finally." She pulls me into her arms, pressing me against her soft, round curves. Malcolm and Sherée's hugs were short and friendly while Hadley's is the kind of hug you give a long-lost friend.

"Where's Lina?" Evan asks just as Jasper enters the kitchen.

"She called a while ago to say her plans had changed and she and her boyfriend will be here tomorrow," Jasper says.

"Don't you mean *Laurelina*?" Malcolm says in an affected snooty accent of some sort. He and Sherée have returned to their seats; they're sitting so close, a sliver of light couldn't pass between their bodies. He turns to Evan and adds, "Remember when the Perry name was good enough for our dear sister and she was just Lina Perry?"

Laurelina Peregrine is the pen name their older sister adopted when she self-published her debut romance novel last year. According to Evan, the book was an unprecedented success, hit multiple bestseller lists, won a bunch of awards, and got Lina an agent and a publishing deal for two more books. Evan says she's always been a bit snobby, but the success made her insufferable and now all she talks about is her book. Out of all of his siblings, Lina was the one I was most wary to meet, so I can't say I'm too upset she won't be joining us until tomorrow.

Jasper clears his throat loudly. "Yes, well, Lina has had great success with her writing, and we mustn't make her feel bad. Plenty of people write under pseudonyms these days. We need to be sure she knows how proud we are of her."

Evan and Malcolm make identical non-committal noises. As I nudge Evan in the ribs, I see Sherée do the same to Malcolm from the corner of my eye. She and I catch each other's gazes and laugh, which sets off everyone else except for Jasper, who releases a long-suffering sigh.

"We'll make sure she knows, Jasper," Evan says. As an aside to me, he adds, "Mostly because she'll fish for compliments." Before I can elbow him again, he chuckles and wraps his arm around me, pinning one of my arms against his side while clutching my other hand against his chest. After pressing a kiss to my forehead, he sweeps his gaze around the kitchen. "Speaking of people who are missing, where's your boyfriend, Hads?"

Hadley hops up on the kitchen island and rifles through the sea of overflowing reusable cloth bags on the counter. Jasper clears his throat loudly and she ignores him. As she continues her perusal, I get the impression she's avoiding making eye contact with Evan. "Tucker is upstairs on the phone. He'll be down in a bit."

Hadley's and Lina's boyfriends are the only ones Evan didn't have index cards for. Hadley spent most of this year traveling through Europe, and when she got back a few months ago, she settled in Toronto and started dating a guy named Tucker. The fact she hasn't told Evan much about him has been a sore spot for him, especially since the pair have always been close. I'm not sure whether he was reassured or more worried when I pointed out their relationship must be serious if she was bringing him on the yearly family Christmas getaway.

Jasper clears his throat again and moves toward the island. Hadley digs through the bags faster and lets out a triumphant cry when she pulls a box of Candy Cane Viva Puffs from the bag.

"Those are for later," Jasper says. "I got the last two boxes at the grocery store, so they'll have to last all week."

"But they're my favorite," Hadley says with a pout.

"Yes, I know, which is why I bought them."

"But nobody else really likes them," she says. "So you should let me have this box and we'll put the other one in the cupboard for everyone else to share." She flashes him a wide, toothy smile. When his face remains impassive, she bats her lashes.

Jasper's rigid shoulders sag a fraction. "Fine, take them. But get off the counter. I have to prepare our meals there, you know."

Hadley plants a loud kiss on Jasper's cheek and slides off the island. The youngest two Perry siblings sure know how to get their way. She gives me a cheeky wink as she passes, tilting her head toward the kitchen door. "Come on you two, I'll show you to your room." As we troop out of the kitchen and follow her up the stairs, she says, "There are two bedrooms downstairs and three upstairs. We put Mal and Sherée downstairs because they go at it like bunnies and they are *not* quiet. When Lina called to say she'd be late, we decided she and her boyfriend could have the other downstairs bedroom."

Evan lets out a loud laugh. We follow Hadley down the hall, past two closed bedroom doors and a bathroom. "I'm surprised Jasper didn't offer to switch."

"Oh, he did. Two of the three bedrooms upstairs have twin beds, though. Yours is the only one with a double."

"And you didn't take that one for yourself?"

Hadley chooses this moment to open the box of cookies she's been carrying, effectively avoiding eye contact with either of us. "Tucker and I aren't quite there in our relationship yet," she says quietly, glancing over her shoulder toward one of the closed doors. "So the twin beds are actually perfect."

Before either of us can comment on that tidbit of information, Hadley holds the box of cookies out to me. I can't resist the scent of chocolate and peppermint, so I snag two.

"You and I have to sneak in a movie night at some point this week," Hadley says to me, taking a cookie and biting into it. "Evan tells me you love any and all Christmas movies, so we'll see how many we can watch."

"What about me?" Evan asks.

Hadley lifts one shoulder and scrunches her face, although her eyes are twinkling with mischief. "You can come too, I guess."

As the two of them fall into familiar jokes and bickering, exchanging pokes and shoves, I lean against the wall, watching in amusement. I may not be an expert on big families, but all our interactions so far have seemed pretty normal. I think Evan let his nerves get the best of him these last few weeks. And who knows, maybe subconsciously he was as nervous about his family meeting me as he was about me meeting them.

Either way, I'm looking forward to this time with the Perry clan, and I'm excited to get the festivities under way.

CHAPTER TWO

I'm in that weird state between asleep and awake where your surroundings somehow work their way into dreams and turn everything to chaos. Someone is banging a door repeatedly while someone else sings loudly. A disembodied male voice drones on, but I can't make out what it's saying.

"Normal people sleep in when they're on holiday. Not the Perrys, though. Nope."

These groggy, muttered words come from beside me in bed. I open my eyes and meet Evan's heavy-lidded gaze. I stare at him for a minute as the dream fades and reality seeps in. I don't hear anyone singing like in my dream, although there are voices and the general clatter of people moving around, likely in the kitchen if the faint scent of coffee is any indication.

Evan stretches out his arm and I snuggle against him, resting my head on his chest. "What time is it?"

"Not even nine." He kisses the top of my head and runs his hand slowly up and down my back. "I naively thought that with you here, they'd be a bit more considerate and let us sleep in. Guess not."

"It's okay," I say around a huge yawn. It *would* have been nice to sleep in a bit more since we both have to get up early every morning for work. Evan doesn't need any extra ammunition, though, so I keep that thought to myself. "Since we're awake, we can put our time to good use."

"Oh yeah?" Even without being able to see his face, I can hear the raised-eyebrow-and-grin combo in his voice.

"Mmhmm. We can get some quality snuggling time in."

His hand freezes on my back. After a beat, a low laugh rumbles under my ear. "Snuggling time. Huh. I had other ideas."

"Oh? Do tell."

"I'd rather show you." In one quick move, I'm on my back and he's hovering over me. While morning breath isn't the sexiest or most romantic thing in the world, we've grown used to each other's after all these months, especially since we both happen to enjoy lazy morning sex when time allows. "We'll have to be quiet," he says, nipping at my bottom lip. When I lift up in an attempt to catch his mouth with mine, he gives me a sly smile and moves to my neck instead. He goes for the sweet spot just under my ear, eliciting a hum of pleasure from me.

I nestle further into the soft, comfortable bed, wrapping my arms around him and spreading my legs wider so our bodies are flush. I let out another little hum as I rock my hips against his. His hand fists in the hem of my shirt before slipping underneath, moving along my stomach until his fingers brush the underside of my breast.

"You guys awake yet? Breakfast is almost ready." The words are accompanied by a loud knock on the door.

My gasp of surprise is followed by Evan's hand jerking out from under my top. I nearly shove him off me so I can bolt under the covers before I remember the door is locked. A shaky laugh escapes me and Evan joins in, rolling off me to flop onto his back.

"I hear you two giggling in there," Hadley calls through the door. "Breakfast is in five and, Evan, you know how Jasper is about us eating together." She taps a jaunty pattern on the door and then her footsteps recede down the hallway.

"Welcome to Christmas vacation, Perry style," Evan says.

※ ※ ※

The irritation of our interrupted sexcapades is soothed somewhat when we arrive downstairs and the scents of sausage, bacon, and pancakes envelope me, making my mouth water.

Jasper is setting a massive platter of pancakes on the table as we enter the kitchen. "Good morning," he says with a tight smile. On anyone else, I'd think the smile was a cover for annoyance, but with Jasper I think it's that he's not used to using those particular muscles frequently.

Malcolm and Sherée are already settled at the table, sitting close and giggling as they whisper to each other. From the satisfied looks on their faces, I'm guessing *they* didn't experience *coitus interruptus* this morning like Evan and I did. Hadley sets a carafe of coffee on the table and takes a seat, motioning for me to sit beside her.

"Where's Tucker?" I ask. We'd been here for nearly an hour yesterday before Hadley's boyfriend finally emerged from their bedroom. Tall and broad with shaggy light-brown hair, he'd shaken Evan's and my hands enthusiastically before launching into a largely one-sided conversation about life in Toronto. He seems nice enough, if a bit loud, over-confident, and basically the exact opposite of Hadley. I don't think Evan was impressed with him; it didn't help that Tucker kept disappearing into the bedroom to take mysterious phone calls throughout the rest of the day.

"He's still sleeping," she says. "I tried to wake him, but he can sleep through anything. He'll be down shortly, I'm sure."

The food is passed around, and coffee and juice are poured. When I compliment Jasper on the feast, he tells me it's tradition for them to start each day during Christmas vacation with a hearty meal.

"We're all normally healthy breakfast eaters," he says, cutting a link of breakfast sausage into bite-size pieces. "Or *non* breakfast eaters," he adds with a pointed glance in Hadley's direction, "but this week is special. Our mother always joked that calories don't count at Christmastime."

"She sounds like my kind of woman." I'm not sure if I should say anything else. I've received all kinds of awkward platitudes in the years since my dad died, so I always hesitate to say them myself because everyone receives them differently. While saying something like *'I wish I'd known your parents'* is true, it could lead the mood into somber territory, and this is supposed to be a celebration.

Evan saves me from my swirl of thoughts. "Our parents would have loved you, Gwen. You too, Sherée."

Malcolm nods, waving a piece of bacon between Sherée and me. "I agree. And they'd love knowing we're all together like this every year."

The sensation of being watched creeps over me. I peer around the table until my gaze settles on Jasper, who's studying me over the rim of his coffee cup.

"Evan tells us your father passed away some years ago," he says, his voice surprisingly gentle.

"Yeah, shortly after I finished college. It was always just the two of us, so it was a devastating loss, which I know you all understand well." It's taken me years—and quite a bit of therapy—to get to a place where I can talk about my dad's death without a rush of emotion overcoming me. "I was really lonely for a long time until I found my work family. And then Evan, of course." At his name, his shoulder bumps mine and his hand settles on my thigh.

"And your mother?" Jasper asks.

"*Jasper.*"

His eyes widen at the warning note in Evan's tone. "I simply want to get to know Gwen better. My apologies if that was rude, it wasn't my intention."

I cover Evan's hand where it still rests on my leg. "It's fine, really. My mother left when I was three. She kept in touch for a few years, but then dropped off the grid. I don't even know where she is these days." That was something else I spent a lot of time working through in therapy, although I'm not sure that's the kind of thing Jasper wants to know.

"How sad," he says. "But you said you have your work family? You work at...what is it, an amusement park?"

"Of sorts, yes. It used to be called Santa's Village, and it was only open a few months of the year. Now it's Bellevue Family Village, and it's open year-round with dozens of shops, restaurants, rides, games, that sort of thing. I'm part of the PR and marketing team."

"She runs all their social media," Evan says proudly. "Their followers have tripled since she took over."

"Don't tell Lina that or she'll be after you for tips," Hadley says. "She's obsessed with her number of followers. She hired an assistant to take over so she could focus on writing, but she still does most of it because she's a control freak."

When Jasper opens his mouth to speak, Hadley holds up a hand to cut him off. "It's true and you know it. The two of you are the same: you both have to be in charge of everything." They lock eyes and have what appears to be a silent war of words across the table. Jasper looks away first, his gaze dropping to the last few morsels of his breakfast.

I wait for tension to settle over the breakfast table. Thankfully Jasper recovers quickly and goes back to asking me questions. I begin to wonder if Evan didn't tell his siblings anything about me this past year, but when Jasper rises to refill the pitcher of orange juice, Evan leans in and whispers, "I told him most of this stuff already, but this is how he is. He likes to get information from the source and store it away in color-coded files in that big ol' brain of his."

I tilt my head closer to him, inhaling the familiar scent of his citrus-and-spice shampoo. "I feel like I'm being interviewed."

"Get used to it. I'm his brother and I sometimes still feel that way. He's a facts-and-figures man."

After breakfast, Hadley is quick to offer Jasper help with cleaning up. Evan, Malcolm, Sherée, and I make our way to the living room. The other couple squeeze into an armchair by the fire, where they immediately wrap themselves around each other and start making out. Evan wasn't kidding when he said they couldn't keep their hands off each other.

He catches my hand and leads me to the armchair furthest away from his brother and sister-in-law. We settle in and he pulls my legs over his lap.

"If you think we're going to get as cozy as they are, you'd better think again," I tell him.

The warm breath from his laughter ruffles my hair. "Don't worry, I know where you draw the line with PDA."

I shoot a quick glance in their direction, afraid to look too closely in case I see something that can't be unseen. "They're really going for it." My gaze jerks back to Evan's when Malcolm's hand disappears up the front of Sherée's shirt.

Expecting Evan to still have that amused smile on his face, I'm surprised to see the crease in his brow. At my questioning look, he says, "Hadley has been acting weird. I've told you how distant she's seemed on the phone lately and how we were talking less and less. I hoped my worries would be put to rest once we were together again, but..." He sighs, making patterns on my thigh with his fingertip. "That distance is still there. I don't get it."

"You'll have to try to get her on her own at some point soon," I tell him. "Maybe if you're alone without distractions, she'll tell you what's going on with her. And if she doesn't, you'll just have to ask her point blank."

He bobs his head slowly. "You're right. I'll try to do it today so it's not hanging over me. Maybe I can pull her aside at the Christmas tree farm if you don't mind?"

"That's a good idea. She can escape to her room here, but there's nowhere for her to go at the farm. I'll distract Tucker while you talk to her."

This gets the desired smile from him. "You're the best."

"I thought *you* were the best."

He lifts one shoulder, his eyes shining with laughter. "I am, it's true. We'll share the title. Sometimes."

Our laughter turns into kissing, which doesn't last long. I'm sure I'm not the only one who feels weird making out in the same room where his older brother and sister-in-law are currently sucking face like there's no tomorrow.

Jasper and Hadley emerge from the kitchen a short time later. She doesn't look in our direction as she whispers something to Jasper and then slinks toward the stairs.

Jasper clears his throat and steps further into the room. Malcolm and Sherée peel themselves apart with what looks like a great deal of effort. I nearly laugh out loud at the disheveled state of their hair and clothes, and I can see Evan shaking his head from the corner of my eye.

"Are we ready for the great Christmas tree hunt?" Jasper asks.

"What about Lina?" Malcolm asks.

"When she phoned yesterday, she said we should go ahead without her. Hadley just informed me she and Tucker will be staying behind, so it'll just be the five of us. We can take my rental since it'll fit all of us comfortably and the tree can be strapped on top."

"Wait, what? Why isn't Hads coming?" Evan asks.

"She said she and Tucker don't get much time alone and this seems like a good chance when it's the only time they'll have the house to themselves."

"But she loves choosing the tree." Evan shifts my legs off his lap and hops up from the chair, starting toward the staircase. "I'm going to go talk to her."

Jasper steps into his path, stopping him with a gentle hand to the shoulder. "She said she knew you'd want to try to change her mind, but she's not going. She promised she'll make it up to you later in the week."

Evan's mouth opens and shuts several times without producing any words. Finally, he gives a resigned nod and returns to the armchair. The disappointment on his face makes my heart clench. He's been talking for weeks about how he couldn't wait to see his little sister and spend time with her, how she was the bright spot in the nuttiness of his family. I'm half tempted to go bang on her door and tell her she's coming with us whether she likes it or not, but I don't want to start any drama, especially less than twenty-four hours into our time together.

Jasper claps his hands and jerks his head toward the front hall. "We'll have fun just the five of us, I promise. Let the Perry family Christmas festivities officially begin!"

CHAPTER THREE

Jasper is ready first—no shocker there—and he heads out to his car to start it. Once the rest of us are ready, we all seem to have the same realization simultaneously as we approach the SUV.

"Who's going to sit where?" Evan's voice is barely above a whisper even though there's no way Jasper can hear us from inside the running car.

"We'll sit in the back row and you two can sit in the middle row," Malcolm says.

"And leave Jasper alone up front like our personal chauffeur?"

Malcolm shrugs one shoulder. "So *you* sit with him."

"But that leaves Gwen alone," Evan says.

"That doesn't matter," I say. "Or *I* could sit up front with Jasper. I don't mind."

"We like you too much for that," Sherée says. I give her a questioning look and she says, "It's about a forty-five minute drive to the farm. In that time, Jasper will point out every species of winter-growing plant and any animal we pass, all while driving the exact speed limit, and probably humming along off-key to the radio."

The opening chords of Mariah Carey's "All I Want For Christmas is You" start playing from inside the car. Jasper gives the horn a few quick taps and waves at us through the window.

"Not the radio," Malcolm says. "His personal Christmas playlist. And the humming along? It'll start that way and progress to full-blown singing by the time we reach the farm. You know those high notes Mariah is famous for? Most normal people don't even attempt them, but Jasper gives them his all. Dogs everywhere start howling."

"Glass shatters," Evan adds.

"Eardrums burst," Sherée chimes in.

Despite my best efforts, I can't contain my laughter. They all sound so serious I can't tell if they're joking or not. Regardless, this is the first year Jasper is the only single one among all his siblings. It's one thing when we're all together inside and everyone is talking as a group, but being in a vehicle is different, plus I know Evan won't mind sitting alone. "I'm sure it's not that bad. I'll sit with him and we'll consider it a rite of passage."

"Taking one for the team." Malcolm sounds impressed as he pats me on the shoulder. To Evan, he adds, "You really *have* found a keeper."

The drive is everything they promised it would be, except their dire warnings are actually things I enjoy, especially being a city girl who can't identify the types of most trees and plants. I'm especially thrilled when Jasper points out a pair of deer frolicking through a field. A few minutes later, I'm the one excitedly pointing at a bushy-tailed fox slinking under some bushes.

He also keeps his singing volume at a minimum. I wonder if it's partly due to self-consciousness since he shoots me surreptitious glances whenever he switches from humming to singing. His voice isn't great, but I've certainly heard worse, and his playlist includes all my favorite winter and holiday songs. By the time we reach the Admans' Christmas Tree Farm, I'm feeling all warm and fuzzy toward my boyfriend's oldest brother.

If the rental house was picture perfect, the farm is like something out of a Hallmark movie. We park in a lot that's filled with dozens of other vehicles and make our way through a thin layer of freshly-fallen snow to the entrance.

Some people head straight for the area with the pre-cut trees while others veer off to the stands where hot drinks and baked goods are available. The scent of pine mixed with chocolate, cinnamon, and peppermint hangs in the air.

"You're like a walking heart-eyes emoji right now," Evan says, looping his arm around my shoulder and pressing his warm lips to my cheek. "I've been to a lot of Christmas tree farms and stands over the years, but this place is unreal."

It reminds me of Bellevue Family Village, where I work. It goes back to its roots as Santa's Village every holiday season, becoming a winter wonderland that draws in tourists from miles around. The tour guides dress as elves, every shop and eatery gets its halls decked with boughs of holly, and the North Pole is revived, giving people a chance to visit Santa seven days a week leading up to Christmas. I don't see any elves running around here, but I do see a lot of enthusiastic, rosy-cheeked faces, and enough decorations to fill our rental house a dozen times over.

I'm debating whether to start at the hot chocolate stand or the area set up with elaborate wreaths when Jasper steps into my line of sight. I don't get a chance to ask for his opinion before he claps his hands and surveys our small group with a determined look.

"All right, gang, are we ready to pick our tree?" Without waiting for a response, he pivots and walks away.

I guess my sugar fix will have to wait. Maybe once we choose our tree, I can pick a wreath that matches. Jasper seems like the type to want a cohesive aesthetic. That doesn't stop me from enviously eyeing the little girl who's passing by with a cup of hot chocolate that's topped with a mountain of whipped cream and green and red sprinkles.

With a longing sigh, I move in the direction of the pre-cut trees. Evan tugs on my hand and shakes his head. "Those trees aren't good enough for Jasper," he says. "Part of the whole Perry family Christmas experience is trudging into the woods and selecting the perfect tree."

"Oh. Well, that sounds fun."

He makes a non-committal noise as he adjusts my scarf, his cool fingers brushing my neck and making me shiver. His lips curl in a knowing smile before descending to cover mine in a brief kiss.

Jasper calls to us, telling us to 'come along'. Evan rolls his eyes and mutters something about us not being children or dogs. The others are waiting at a small wooden hut where a man in a plaid shirt and puffy Admans' Tree Farm vest is taking a clipboard and pen back from Jasper.

"You're all set, folks," the man says, giving us a quick smile as we join our group. "There are employees circulating the property to make sure everyone stays safe and has help if they need it. Once you've cut down your tree, find a worker in one of these red vests, and they'll bring the tree back here to get it fixed up and taken to your car."

"Excellent. Thank you kindly." Jasper pulls a pair of thick gloves from his coat pocket and dons them as he follows the man around to the side of the hut. When he returns, he's carrying an old blanket and a saw. "And we're off," he says to us, marching purposefully toward the wooded area that's marked off for tree cutting.

Just before we disappear into the trees, the sound of jingling bells draws my attention to a trail where a horse-drawn sleigh is emerging, carrying a load of people. I swallow a groan. I understand Jasper is single-minded and we'll likely do all the fun stuff after we pick our tree, but having to pass through it all first is a tease.

"You should tell Hugh and Ivy they need to up their game at the Village next Christmas," Evan says, referring to my bosses, who are also good friends of ours and the ones who set us up last New Year's Eve.

"We actually discussed it in the fall before the Village switched to Christmas mode," I tell him. "We decided there wasn't really enough room to do it safely, though."

"You and your big beautiful brain, always one step ahead of me." He slings his arm around my shoulder and pulls me close to his side, pressing a kiss to my forehead.

"The credit goes to Hallmark and Pinterest in this case. I was doing some research, looking for new ways to wow the Christmas crowds. The sleigh rides would have been a nice touch."

"Like that episode of *Gilmore Girls* where they have the festival and do sleigh rides in the snow," Evan says, giving me a squeeze.

I laugh under my breath, watching the fog mingle with the wispy air from Evan's breaths. When we first got together, we made each other watch all the shows and movies that defined our childhood and teen years. Evan's pick was the *Star Wars* movies and mine was *Gilmore Girls*. While he was hesitant at first, he quickly became addicted to the series and was always asking for 'one more episode'. Our already-strong bond was cemented over late nights in Stars Hollow with the Gilmores.

As we head into a more heavily wooded area and the lingering scent of frost mixed with trees perfumes the air, excitement bubbles up inside me. I've never had a real Christmas tree, let alone been to a lot or a farm. My dad and I had a fake tree we hauled out of storage every December. After he died, I kept most of our decorations and donated the tree to a charity shop. Every year since, I've put a few decorations up in my apartment, but I never did get another tree. There didn't seem to be any point since I was on my own.

"Maybe next year we could get an artificial tree to put up in the apartment," I say. We're trailing a few feet behind Malcolm and Sherée, with Jasper leading the charge somewhere up ahead. "There's no sense getting a real one since we'll be gone over the holidays with your family, but we could enjoy it in the weeks leading up to Christmas and into the new year."

Evan keeps his gaze on the uneven ground, but I don't miss the soft, sweet smile lifting his lips. "Yeah. Yeah, let's definitely do that. My family is pretty set on their traditions, but we should create some of our own too. Stuff we can pass down if...y'know,
if we have kids someday. And even if we don't, it'd be nice to have our own traditions, just the two of us."

"Fake Christmas trees, yearly *Gilmore Girls* marathons..."

He chuckles. "All of that and a million other little things."

Our one-year anniversary is coming up in less than two weeks. When we moved in together six months ago, we agreed we both knew we were in this relationship for the long haul, and would have the 'big discussions' someday soon. Between work and our busy social lives, those discussions still haven't happened yet, other than an agreement neither of us is anywhere near ready for kids.

Before Evan, I'd never been serious enough with anyone to contemplate marriage. Even if I had been, I was turned off the idea from a young age; most of my close friends' parents were divorced and I saw what it did to them, especially when it came to custody battles. Despite my own parents never getting married, my dad confessed to me once that he didn't think my mother would have stuck around even if they *had* been married. She didn't like to be tied down.

When Evan walked into my life and our whirlwind romance led to him being a permanent fixture within weeks of us meeting, I realized I'd be happy being married or not, as long as we were together. If I were to go back in time to exactly one year ago now and tell myself I'd soon be the happiest I've ever been, contemplating the appeal of a sparkly engagement ring and an exchange of vows, I'd never believe it. Past Me was happily single and didn't care about any of those things.

"What's with the little grin?" Evan asks.

"Just thinking about how much life can change in a year," I tell him. "And how ridiculously happy I am."

He pulls me to a stop, his gloved hands cupping my face. I expect him to kiss me, but he wraps his arms around me instead, hugging me tight. I close my eyes and breathe in his familiar scent, changed only slightly by the added smell of his wool coat.

A loud whistle pierces the air. I jump in Evan's arms, but he just sighs and slowly releases me. "Jasper," he says, as if that explains everything. I peer over his shoulder to see Malcolm and Sherée pulling apart after what looks like yet another hot and heavy make-out session. Jasper is standing a few feet beyond them looking exasperated.

"Why don't we divide and conquer," he says as we join the others. My gaze slides to Sherée, who's dabbing at her mouth with her fingers in an attempt to smooth her smudged lipstick. We lock eyes—hers a bit dazed from lust—and share a little grin. I tune back into Jasper as he's telling Evan and Malcolm to give the Perry signal if any of us find the perfect tree.

"What's the Perry signal?" I ask Evan as we head off in the opposite direction from where Jasper is going.

He rolls his eyes. "That loud whistle you just heard." He sticks his thumb and forefinger in his mouth to illustrate, although thankfully he doesn't blow.

"Wow. That's…"

"Obnoxious? Yeah. I mean, it has its uses, but for the most part it just annoys people. He taught Hadley and me how to do it after our parents died in case we got lost when we were out together." He must notice I'm trying not to laugh because he gives a wry smile. "Yes, we were fifteen and sixteen when our parents died. I wasn't kidding all those times I told you how seriously Jasper took his role as our guardian."

"Malcolm had already moved out by the time your parents died, hadn't he?"

Evan nods. "Jasper taught him anyway *'just in case'*," he says, making air quotes around the words.

I have no idea why the image makes me laugh, yet it does. Evan joins in and we keep giggling as we link arms and traipse down the gravel path. Neither of us pays much attention to the trees; I think we're both enjoying our few moments of alone time, knowing they'll be few and far between in the next several days.

"I wish Hadley had come with us." Evan's voice is quiet, like he's making a confession. "And I wish I knew what was going on with her. All of my siblings are pretty predictable—they always act the same, nothing ever changes with them, not really. You can count on Malcolm to be sarcastic and Jasper to be over-the-top with his need for control. You can count on Lina to make literally anything and everything about herself."

I pull him to a stop and turn him so we're facing each other, holding hands.

"Hadley has always been on the quiet side," he continues. "Even though she prefers to do her own thing, her sense of family obligation is strong and she knows family togetherness means a lot to Jasper. To *all* of us when it comes right down to it. If it were just the fact she didn't come today I could get over it, but she's been acting weird for months. She used to tell me everything, come to me for advice, call me out of the blue for absolutely no reason other than to touch base. Ever since she got back from Europe I've felt like she's been avoiding me, and now I'm sure she is." He sighs heavily, shaking his head.

Evan has always shared his emotions freely; it's one of the things I love best about him. He wears his heart on his sleeve and he's not afraid to show you how he feels. The hurt and disappointment written across his face now are like a knife to the heart. I can feel his pain and I have no idea how to make it better. "Maybe when we get home—"

"There you are," Jasper says breathlessly, appearing from around a group of trees. "Any luck?"

A quick glance at Evan tells me he's not in the mood to deal with Jasper right now, so I step forward and point to the tree closest to us. "How about this one? It's a good height and has nice...umm...branches."

Jasper makes a humming sound as he circles the tree, eyes narrowed. From the way he's inspecting the thing, you'd think the fate of the world depends on his decision. Finally he stops and shakes his head, lips pursed. "I don't think so. It's not quite tall enough and the branches don't have the right symmetry. It also looks a little dry. We chose a dry tree one year and we all tracked needles throughout the house for days. They're a bugger to vacuum up, let me tell you. And..." He gives the tree one last critical look. "This is a spruce. We're really more of a fir family. A nice first attempt, though, Gwen." He pats my shoulder, shoots a curious glance in his brother's direction, and then disappears wherever he came from.

I'm rooted to the spot, blinking after him. Evan comes up behind me and wraps his arms around my stomach, resting his chin on my shoulder. "Congratulations. You've just been Jaspered."

I free myself from him and spin around to face him. He arranges his features into a mask of sympathy, but I can see the laughter in his eyes. "He...I...he could have just said 'let's keep looking' instead of giving a freakin' dissertation on why the tree sucks. What if I'd actually picked that tree and had my heart set on it? I don't think he meant to be condescending, but that pat on the shoulder and basically telling me 'nice try'? Seriously?"

Evan is shaking with suppressed laughter now. I give him a shove and he stumbles back, the laughter spilling out. "I'm sorry, I'm sorry. I know you've thought I was being too hard on him all this time and maybe even exaggerating, but now you see."

"I'm glad you find this so amusing." Despite sounding huffy, even *I* can't stop my lips from twitching. "I was starting to feel the warm fuzzies toward him after our drive here, but they're quickly disappearing after *that*."

He approaches me slowly, hands up like I'm a wild animal who will bite at the least provocation. I roll my eyes and step forward, allowing him to wrap his arms around me. "You know how you said earlier that riding up front with Jasper was a rite of passage? *This* was the real test. Welcome to the family."

I try to shove him away again, but he holds on tighter. "Careful, or my warm fuzzy feelings for *you* will start disappearing too." Despite my words, I nestle against him, adjusting his scarf so my face doesn't rub against the rough wool of his coat.

Another whistle rips through the air. Evan tucks his face into my neck and whispers that it's Jasper. We remain as we are, neither of us moving for several more minutes. When we do finally release each other and start toward where the sound came from, we share a secret smile.

We get a bit turned around in the labyrinthine paths trying to find Jasper and the others. I'm tempted to shout 'Marco' and see if Jasper responds with 'Polo'. When I mention this to Evan, he assures me his brother has likely moved on to another tree, otherwise he would have whistled again.

A moaning sound up ahead has our steps slowing. We've passed a few red-vested Admans' Tree Farm employees, who I'm sure would have noticed if someone was hurt along the paths. Still, I veer in that direction, tugging Evan along with me. A muffled gasp has me picking up speed. I'm about to turn onto the path where the noise is coming from when Evan pulls on my hand and hisses at me to wait. I heed his warning too late and get an eyeful of Malcolm and Sherée tucked between two tall trees, playing tonsil hockey and practically dry humping through their many layers of clothes.

In my haste to back away, I trip on a stump and fall into Evan's arms. Without missing a beat, he hauls me back around the corner out of sight of his brother and sister-in-law. By the time I'm back on my feet, we're both trying so hard to suppress our laughter, we can hardly stand up straight.

"My eyes!" I whisper-yell, covering my face.

"We're going to have to fit those two with bells," Evan says.

"Hey, guys," Malcolm calls through the trees.

"This is a family establishment," Evan says, raising his voice so they can hear. "You two need to get a room and stay there."

They emerge onto our path, still straightening their jackets. I expect them to look sheepish, but they're wearing matching *'what can you do?'* expressions.

"Believe me, we'd rather be locked away together in a room than freezing our asses off out here," Malcolm says. "Especially when we all know Jasper doesn't care about our opinions."

As if summoned, Jasper appears. He seems to do that a lot. Despite my earlier irritation with him, I hope he didn't hear what Malcolm just said. My gaze moves over him, taking in the fact the blanket and saw he was carrying are gone.

"Our tree has been cut and is being taken up as we speak," he says, clapping his hands together. The motion draws my attention to his gloved hands, which are glistening with sap around the fingertips. "Shall we head back?" The question is obviously rhetorical because he pivots and starts marching back toward the front of the farm.

My gaze swings to Evan. He quickly rearranges his features from a cringe to a forced smile as our eyes meet. "Umm..."

"You didn't warn her?" Malcolm asks.

"Warn me about what?"

"Why don't we start back?" Sherée says to Malcolm, jerking her head in the direction Jasper went.

"Don't get sidetracked this time," Evan tells them as they walk away, arms slung around each other. To me he says, "Okay, so, Jasper pretty much always chooses the tree himself. It goes back to that whole 'he's always right, his opinion is the only one that matters' thing I told you about." He steps closer and grips my shoulders, kneading them through my heavy coat. "I should have warned you, but...sometimes I forget you haven't always been part of the family since it *feels* like we've known each other forever."

His sweet words ease some of my—what? Surprise? Annoyance? I'm not quite sure how to pinpoint what I'm feeling.

Before I can speak, he says, "I've learned over the years to pick my battles. Would I like a say in our Christmas tree? Sure, but it doesn't really matter in the grand scheme of things. I'm not a perfectionist like Jasper. I don't really care what the tree itself looks like, but it makes him happy for all of us to traipse out here together. Next year, we'll get our own tree and even if it *is* artificial it'll be something we picked out together, and something we can enjoy for many Christmases to come."

He's right. Jasper's need for control is how he is and it doesn't hurt me. Evan, Malcolm, and even Sherée are all used to it and don't seem to care, and I'm sure I'll adjust too. "I want our fake tree to be a spruce," I say, looping my arms around his neck.

His warm breath washes over my face with his laughter as he leans in to rub his nose against mine. "Deal."

On the way back to the front of the farm I contemplate my choice of drinks from the stands. Hot chocolate? Hot apple cider? Maybe I could get one and talk Evan into the other so we can share. I'm about to tell him this when I see Jasper's SUV up ahead with a netting-wrapped tree being strapped to the roof.

Jasper waves when he sees us. The sight of a rare smile on his face eases my clenched muscles until he calls, "We're all set! Let's hit the road!"

"But...but..." I glance longingly toward the food and drink stands. The wreaths. The sleigh rides! And crap, are those warm pretzels? "What the hell is the point of driving forty-five minutes if we're not going to enjoy everything the farm has to offer?" I ask Evan. "We're supposed to be on holiday. Is a schedule really that important?"

"To Jasper, yes," Malcolm says from a few feet away.

"But I want hot chocolate. And a pretzel." My tone sounds petulant even to my own ears and I fear I'm dangerously close to a pout. "Think I can run over there and get them to go?"

The sound of Malcolm's low chuckle reaches my ears as he and Sherée walk toward the SUV. I look at Evan, who's cringing yet again. "Jasper doesn't allow food and drink in the car?" The words come out tentatively, sounding like a question. At my huff, he takes my hand and turns me away from the stands. "Remember, pick your battles. That irritation you're feeling will fade and you'll learn to roll your eyes, shake your head, and go with it like the rest of us."

We've reached the SUV now. Jasper is already in the driver's seat and Malcolm is about to open the back door. Sherée turns to me and says, "He's right. I jumped on the bitter train my first Christmas with these guys because this is *not* how my family works. But my family also doesn't care a lick about Christmas, so it balances out in an odd sort of way. You'll get used to it. These guys make it worth the hassle." She pats Evan's cheek lovingly and turns to kiss Malcolm before climbing into the car.

"I promise I'll make you hot chocolate when we get back to the house," Evan whispers. "I'll even spike it with peppermint schnapps."

Now he's talking. Still, the warm fuzzies I was feeling toward Jasper have evaporated in the last hour. When Evan asks where I'm sitting for the ride home, I choose the backseat with him.

CHAPTER FOUR

❋

Lina and her boyfriend still haven't arrived by the time we get back to the house. Malcolm helps Jasper bring the tree inside while Evan dashes upstairs, calling over his shoulder that he needs to make a quick phone call.

With the tree taking pride of place in the living room, I have to admit Jasper made a good choice. It's tall and full, and the scent mixes with the mulled wine he put in the slow cooker this morning to create a wonderfully homey, Christmassy aroma.

"We can decorate the tree tonight or tomorrow, depending on when Lina gets here," Jasper says. "It'll give it time to fall out."

Evan returns downstairs with Hadley and Tucker in tow. Jasper goes off to make lunch, politely declining my help, and the rest of us gather in the living room. When Hadley suggests a movie, I expect a lot of back and forth and arguing about what to watch, but she puts *The Santa Clause* on and everyone settles in to watch it.

"This is always the first Christmas movie we watch as a family," Evan whispers to me as the opening piano chords of 'Oh Christmas Tree' start playing on the TV's speakers. "It was the first movie our parents took us all to see in the theater. Hadley's and my first ever theater experience."

"My dad took me to see it too," I tell him. "It's always been one of my favorites. The child in me loves the first one best, but the adult in me secretly prefers the second one."

He wraps his arm around me and I burrow against his side. "Let me guess, it's because of the romance in the second one?"

"You know me so well."

He kisses my forehead. "That I do. And I love the second one too. Hadley and I went to see it together the year—" He's interrupted by his phone buzzing in his pocket. He shoots me an apologetic look as he untangles himself from my limbs and sits up to check his phone. I catch Hugh's name on the screen before he angles it away from me. It's a subtle move, but I notice it immediately because there are no secrets between us.

"Everything okay?" I ask.

"Umm, yeah." His eyes dart away from mine. He grips his phone tightly and scooches to the edge of the couch. "I'll be back, 'kay?" Without waiting for me to respond, he hurries from the room, answering his phone before he reaches the stairs.

Jasper surfaces from the kitchen a few minutes later carrying several old-school TV trays. He motions for Hadley to pause the movie, which she does, and then he unfolds the trays and places them in front of where each of us is sitting.

"If I let you eat lunch in here so we can watch the movie, will you all promise to be careful?"

"Considering we're a group of thirty-somethings and not preschoolers, I think we can manage," Malcolm says.

"I don't know, I *have* often thought you could stand to wear a bib," Sherée says.

Malcolm's mouth drops open and he sputters out a laugh. "Do you *want* to sit at the table and try to make pleasant conversation for half an hour?"

"No, I want to keep watching the movie. I'm just saying, don't be surprised if you find a bib or two in your stocking this year." She catches my eye and sends me a cheeky wink.

"Tell Santa to add one to Evan's stocking too," I say.

"What am I getting in my stocking?" Evan asks, coming back into the room.

"Coal," Sherée says without missing a beat. "Now let's eat."

After we've eaten a delicious lunch of minestrone soup and crusty bread and finished watching the movie, Hadley says it's time to get out the games.

"Scrabble?" Jasper asks hopefully.

"*No!*" his siblings all shout at once.

At my bewildered expression, Evan says, "He's like a walking dictionary. He always uses words none of us have even heard of before, so there's no hope in hell of any of us winning."

"You and Lina can play if she ever gets here," Malcolm says, clapping Jasper on the shoulder. "Now, Pictionary or Charades?"

A debate ensues, and we finally put it to a vote. Hadley, Sherée, and I vote for Pictionary—"I can't draw for shit, but I'm not making a fool of myself acting stuff out" was Sherée's reasoning—while Evan, Malcolm, and Tucker vote for Charades.

"Jasper, you didn't vote," Evan says.

"You all know I'm terrible at both games," he says, practically wringing his hands.

"How about a nice game of Kerplunk instead? Or perhaps a card game? Something quieter, preferably where I don't get yelled at for my incompetence in acting or drawing?"

Part of me wants to laugh while the other part feels sorry for him. Everyone promises to take it easy on him and he finally caves and votes for Pictionary. We pick teams using the Official Perry Method: team captains are nominated at random and everyone else stands in a circle while the first team captain spins around, eyes closed, and picks the members of their team. Everyone else is on the other team. Evan and I somehow get chosen as captains, and I'm the lucky one who gets to spin around blindly and choose my team. From the laughter around me, I'm guessing this is some sort of Perry hazing ritual as much as anything. I end up with Jasper, Sherée, and Tucker.

"What should we call our team?" Sherée asks as we huddle together to talk strategy.

"The Outsiders!" Tucker says immediately. "Since we're all partners of Perrys." His gaze settles on Jasper. "Oops, never mind. Sorry, bro."

"Actually, The Outsiders seems quite apropos," Jasper says dryly.

"Huh?"

"Fitting," Sherée says. Tucker still looks confused, but she moves on. "Are any of you good at drawing? We should try to start strong."

We decide Sherée will go first. When we reconvene with the others, it's decided we'll do a Christmas-themed game in the spirit of the holidays. We all write down a bunch of prompts on scraps of paper and stuff them into one of the stockings by the fireplace.

Within the first ten minutes of playing, I realize two things: there isn't a single artist among us, and Tucker has one of the worst cases of squirrel brain I've ever seen. The minute someone starts drawing, he hops around, blurting things at random. When Jasper gets 'North Pole' as a prompt and starts drawing an actual pole, Tucker shouts, "A candy cane! Santa's cane! Wait, Santa doesn't have a cane, does he? A Christmas dildo!"

Sherée and I collapse against each other, laughing so hard we can't get out any coherent words, leaving poor Jasper red-faced and Tucker continuing to shout ridiculous guesses.

I call a break after that, saying I'm going to pee my pants if I don't go to the bathroom before we continue. When I come back downstairs, the chatter that filled the room when I left has turned into hushed voices and muffled giggles. I round the corner to find everyone crowded around Evan, who's showing them something on his phone.

"Okay, what am I missing?" I ask.

Everyone scuttles away, avoiding my gaze. Evan remains in the center of the room, tucking his phone into his pocket. A hint of color blooms in his cheeks. He sends a quick glance toward his brothers, and Malcolm gives him a nod of encouragement.

I'm about to repeat my question when Evan strides toward me, putting an arm around my waist and guiding me from the room. "I have a surprise for you," he says, ushering me upstairs to our bedroom. "I was trying to get it all sorted out without you knowing, but I don't like keeping things from you, and I know you were getting suspicious."

"I *was* getting suspicious. You've been all twitchy."

"At least you know I could never keep anything big from you or lie to you."

"True. Does this mean I get to know the surprise now?"

We sit on the bed and he takes my hands. "I know how disappointed you were about not getting to do anything at the Christmas tree farm this morning, so I thought we could go out for dinner tonight just the two of us. It'll get more hectic once Lina arrives, so tonight would be our best bet."

I free my hands from his so I can cup his cheeks. "You're so sweet!" We've both been so busy with work lately, we haven't had a date night in ages. Despite falling immediately into a relationship when we met, we realized the fact we were inseparable didn't mean we should miss out on proper dates. We typically try for at least one night a week, but with work getting busier around the holidays for both of us, it hasn't happened in a month or more. "Where does Hugh come into this, though?"

"You saw that, huh?" He scratches at the stubble on his chin and peers up at me through his lashes. I have a feeling he's not going to tell me the whole truth, but if it means not ruining his surprise completely, I can pretend I don't notice. "You know how Hugh seems to know everyone within a hundred-kilometer radius of Bellevue? Well, I asked him if he knew of any restaurants nearby and could pull some strings to get us a last minute reservation. Thanks to him, we'll be having dinner tonight at a place called La Lune about a ten-minute drive from here."

I give an excited squeal and pounce on him, knocking him flat on his back. He lets out a little *'oof'* as the air is knocked out of him. Before I can apologize, we both start laughing. His hands drift to my hips, then venture south as he kisses me between breathless laughs.

"Later," I tell him, stopping his wandering fingers before they disappear into the waistband of my jeans.

"Later," he echoes, making it sound like a dirty, fun promise. "For now let's get ready to escape the Perry family madness."

❄ ❄ ❄

"We need to make it our mission to find a restaurant like this in or near Bellevue," I tell Evan as our dinner plates are whisked away. "This place is incredible."

Leave it to Hugh to make us reservations at a place straight out of a magazine spread. From the outside, La Lune looks huge, while inside it's divided in a way that makes each table feels private and cozy. The room glows with tiny white lights wound around columns and hanging from the exposed wood rafters, and LED tea light candles flicker from the center of each table. Elegant, understated Christmas decorations are peppered throughout the room, with an enormous tree showcased in the front window beside a stone fireplace.

"We could just come back here," Evan says. "Make a monthly reservation once the weather is nice, and have a little getaway from the city."

"I like the way you think, Mr. Perry."

As he pours the rest of the wine into our glasses, I turn to the window beside our table and admire the view outside. The restaurant is on a quiet street lined with shops, all of which are decked out with greenery and colored lights.

"You really do love this time of year, don't you?" Evan asks.

I can feel the goofy smile on my face as I nod, watching a couple pause in front of the shop across the street to admire the Christmas tree in the front window. "I do. There's just something in the air that feels magical, you know? All the lights and decorations, the music, the wonderfully cheesy movies that make you believe anything is possible even when the world around you sometimes feels anything *but* magical."

"I want this Christmas to be extra special and memorable for you," he says, taking my hand across the table. "And when I say memorable, I don't mean catching my brother and his wife making out at every turn or Hadley's boyfriend screaming 'Christmas dildo' during Pictionary today."

I almost spit out the sip of wine I just took. I laugh into my napkin as I wipe my mouth, and Evan chuckles along with me. "Those things will definitely be memorable, though. As will my first experience *not* getting to choose a Christmas tree."

"Right. See, that's one of the many traits I love about you: your ability to roll with things and laugh about them, even when they're not ideal. I can guarantee you it will get nuttier at the house, especially once Lina arrives. Between that and the fact you haven't had a proper holiday since your dad died, I want to make sure this Christmas is one you'll remember for all the right reasons."

He raises my hand to his mouth and presses his lips against my knuckles. He's been extra affectionate and attentive tonight and I'm not complaining one bit. After a hectic few weeks for both of us, it's nice to feel like the center of each other's universes again. Between his focus on me all evening and the way he's currently absentmindedly rubbing my left ring finger, a little voice in my head has been whispering that perhaps his twitchiness and secret planning tonight is leading to a proposal.

Our server approaches the table and Evan lowers my hand without releasing it. "Can I interest you in some coffee or tea and the dessert menu?" she asks.

I open my mouth to say yes—the couple at the table closest to us is sharing a slice of cheesecake that has my mouth watering—but Evan says, "Not tonight, thanks. We were just saying we're going to make this place a regular date spot, so we'll be sure to leave room next time."

"Fantastic, I'm glad to hear you'll be returning. I'll be back in a minute with your bill."

When she leaves, I squeeze Evan's hand, and not in an affectionate way. "The Perry men seem determined to deprive me of sweets."

He winces. "Sorry, I know it looks that way. I have something else planned for dessert, though."

Somewhat placated, I say, "More surprises, eh? Is this mystery dessert somewhere nearby?"

Evan's lips twitch. "You could say that..."

Our server returns with the check, and she and I chat about Christmas plans while Evan pays. As she takes the card machine back, she points toward the giant tree I've been admiring all night. "We invite all our guests to take an ornament from the tree before they leave," she says. "I do hope we'll see you both again in the new year. Merry Christmas."

Once we're bundled back up in our coats and scarves, we pause at the tree. Most of the ornaments are moon-themed with the restaurant's logo and the year stamped on the back. There are full moons and crescent moons of various sizes and colors; my eye is drawn to a silver crescent moon with a glittery star attached at the bottom.

Evan follows my line of sight and gently plucks the ornament from the tree. "This one?" At my nod, he picks up a small tissue paper-lined box from a basket nearby and nestles it inside. "Perfect. We can hang it from the lamp in our room this week and then put it on our tree next year."

The urge to kiss him is too strong to resist. I keep it short and PG since this is a fancy restaurant, and then I pull him around the other side of the tree and make him snap a few selfies with me with the tree and fireplace in the background.

Outside, the crisp winter air is welcome against my heated cheeks after being so close to the roaring fire. Evan and I link arms and start walking down the sidewalk.

"Any hints about this maybe-nearby place we're getting dessert?" I ask.

"I think it's this way." He points vaguely down the street in the direction we're walking. We took a taxi to the restaurant so we could both enjoy a few glasses of wine without worrying about driving afterward. Because of that and the fact it's a beautiful, clear night, it doesn't matter how far we stray from the restaurant, so I decide to let him be mysterious and see where the night takes us.

We follow the curve of the street and end up in Market Square. Yet another enormous evergreen tree sits in the middle, this one festooned with so many colored lights I bet it's visible from space. People are milling around food stands and gathering near the steps of Town Hall, where a group dressed in Victorian outfits appears to be getting ready to sing.

"Over here," Evan says, leading me in the direction of a hot chocolate stand. I do an internal happy dance, thinking I'm finally about to get the chocolaty goodness I was promised this afternoon...but we reach it and keep walking. I glance longingly over my shoulder, sniffing the air and inhaling the scents of chocolate and peppermint.

Evan comes to a stop and I halt beside him. Up ahead in the puddle of warm yellow light cast by an old-fashioned street lamp is a horse-drawn carriage. The carriage is adorned with green garland and what I'm guessing are battery-operated fairy lights. The driver, dressed in a long wool coat and top hat, stands beside the carriage, watching the crowd with a smile.

I groan. "The universe is taunting me. First the sleigh at the Christmas tree farm and now this."

"Except *this*..." Evan slips his arm from mine to take my hand, giving it a squeeze. "Is for us. *Just* us."

My head whips in his direction. His sweet, soft smile tells me he's serious. "How did you do this?"

He leans in, brushing a kiss on my cheek. With his mouth close to my ear, breath warm against my skin, he whispers, "A little Christmas magic."

My brain doesn't have time to formulate a response before we're walking again. The driver turns to us as we approach, his smile growing.

"Mr. Perry and Ms. Dunwich?"

"That's us," Evan says.

The driver removes his hat and gives us a low, sweeping bow, making his coat billow out around him. I can't stop the delighted laugh that escapes me as he offers me his hand and helps me climb into the carriage. The bench seat is covered in a sea of blankets; I leave some on the seat and pick up an armful to cover us when we sit.

"I think I got everything Mr. MacKinnon requested, but if you need anything at all you just let me know," the driver says.

Evan thanks him and climbs in beside me. I scooch close to him and arrange the blankets around our legs. I wait until the carriage is moving before I ask, "Mr. MacKinnon, huh? You had Hugh's help with this too?"

"I told you he knows everyone within a hundred-kilometer radius of Bellevue," Evan says, snuggling closer. He pulls away just as quickly and leans forward, making a small sound of triumph when he uncovers a picnic basket hidden under a blanket on the bench across from us. He opens it to reveal a Thermos and various takeout containers from a bakery whose name I recognize as one of the businesses we passed on our way to Market Square. "I told him what I wanted to do for you, asked him if he could point me in the right direction, and he said he'd take care of all of it. He said to consider it a Christmas gift from him and Ivy."

"And all we got them was that popcorn maker they wanted," I say, my voice wobbly. I'm afraid I'm seconds away from turning into a blubbering mess. Evan tucks me against his body, peppering my face with light kisses until I'm laughing again.

As the carriage makes its way through town, we enjoy cups of rich hot chocolate (*finally!*) along with a variety of bite-size desserts. My favorites are the peppermint and chocolate macarons, which remind me of Hadley's coveted holiday Viva Puffs. I almost mention it to Evan, but I'm afraid bringing up his sister would be a mood killer since things are so strained between them. This is supposed to be a romantic night for the two of us, so I sit back and enjoy the clip-clop of the horses' hooves and the elaborately decorated houses and businesses around town, all with the man of my dreams nestled beside me.

When we return to Market Square, we thank the driver profusely before calling a taxi to take us home. The house is mostly dark when we pull in and there's an extra car in the driveway that tells us Lina and her boyfriend have finally arrived.

"I think they're watching a movie," Evan says, inclining his chin toward the front window as we approach the house. "I doubt we can sneak by them, but we'll say a quick goodnight and head upstairs if that's okay? I just want to be alone with you." The way he says it, low and with a hint of a growl on the last few words, makes my skin tingle.

We shed our coats and boots as quietly as possible. Evan was right about us not being able to sneak past the others since we have to go through the living room to get to the stairs. The minute we enter the room, the TV goes silent as someone pauses the movie. Jasper is sitting in the armchair closest to the fire, while Hadley and Tucker are curled up on opposite ends of one of the couches.

"How was your date?" Hadley asks.

"Wonderful," I say. "You guys should think about heading into town at some point before you go back to Toronto. The whole place is like a Christmas postcard and there are a bunch of shops and restaurants."

Hadley's face lights up. She looks like she's going to say something, but Tucker asks, "Is there a bar in town? Or a nightclub?"

The smile slips off Hadley's face as her gaze goes to the paused TV screen. Evan says, "Uh, we passed a saloon on the outskirts of town. Looked pretty popular." Tucker nods without saying anything else, so Evan turns his attention to Jasper. "Lina's finally here?"

"Yes, she and Van arrived about an hour ago. They said they'd had a long day and went straight to their room. Malcolm and Sherée have gone to bed early too."

"I think we'll turn in too," Evan says quickly. "Gotta get rested up before more Christmassy fun tomorrow. Enjoy the movie, guys."

He ushers me out of the room while the others say goodnight to our retreating forms. We veer toward the stairwell, nearly colliding with Sherée on her way out of the kitchen. She lets out a squeak, which I assume is because we scared her...until my eyes adjust and I realize she's wearing nothing but one of Malcolm's sweaters, and carrying what looks like a can of whipped cream.

"Busted," she whispers. The two of us start giggling while Evan groans and averts his gaze from his half-naked sister-in-law. She grips my arm and slinks past me, saying over her shoulder, "Enjoy your night, you two."

"I obviously don't need to tell you to do the same," I whisper back. I can hear her laughing again as she slips into her bedroom down the hall.

Evan closes his eyes and massages his temples. "Okay, scrubbing that image from my brain. I'll never look at whipped cream the same way again."

"Not even if I wanted to do what they're clearly about to do?" I ask, pulling him toward the stairs.

He shakes his head so hard I bet it makes his brain rattle. "No. No, because they *clearly* took a pie into their bedroom and they're about to have dessert. There is absolutely *no other reason* Sherée would have that whipped cream."

In our room, we barely get the door closed before I push him against it and press my lips to his neck. Between kisses, I say, "Did you notice Hadley and Tucker were sitting about as far apart as they could get?"

Evan grips my hips, yanking me closer. "You really need to stop talking about my siblings." In a flash, he reverses our positions, pressing me against the door and dipping down to nip my earlobe with his teeth. "I don't want to think about anything except you right now."

"I'm okay with that." My voice comes out breathy as his mouth moves over my throat. Even after all this time, he still has the ability to make me weak at the knees and set my pulse thrumming. He hasn't even touched me yet and I'm already aching for him.

He crushes his mouth to mine as we stagger across the room, our lips parting long enough to remove each other's shirts. His mouth moves hungrily across my neck and shoulders, open-mouthed kisses mixed with gentle presses of his lips. My bra joins our shirts on the floor, followed quickly by the rest of our clothes.

We fall onto the mattress together, laughing as the bed makes a sound somewhere between a screech and a moan. I don't have time to say I hope the others didn't hear it before I'm lost in sensation, our limbs tangling, hands reaching and grasping.

"I love you, Gwen. I love you so much."

My gasped reply is barely coherent as his fingers move from my breast down my stomach. My muscles quiver, knowing what's coming next. I bury my face in his shoulder to muffle my cries when his searching fingers find their target.

There's always been something like magic between us. I've never voiced it to anyone because it seems unbelievable and maybe overly romantic, but it's true. I had been with a few guys before Evan, and while I'd enjoyed sex for the most part, I had never experienced that transcendental feeling you read about in books or see on screen. But right from the first time with Evan, it was different. He knew how to touch me and wasn't afraid to take direction. We mapped and memorized each other's bodies until each of us could play the other like a finely tuned instrument. That transcendental feeling that was always out of my grasp before has been a regular part of my life over the last year, as have countless mind-numbing orgasms.

One of those orgasms is creeping up on me now, making my vision blur and darken around the edges. All I have to do is say his name and he knows; he removes his hand from between my legs and lets me grip his hard length, giving him a few slow strokes before guiding him inside me.

His mouth moves over mine in a hot, wet slide as he enters me. Our bodies rock together, quickly finding their usual rhythm. I wrap my legs around his waist and run my hands over his back, fingers digging and nails scratching whenever his thrusts hit me just right.

A soft whimper escapes me when he slows the pace. Supporting himself on one forearm, he grips my hip with his free hand and angles me upward, rotating his hips so he hits my clit with each thrust. I let out a sharp cry and immediately clap a hand over my mouth. Evan's movements falter for a second and his eyes shine with mirth as he releases my hip to pry my hand away from my mouth.

He keeps my hand grasped in his as we get back in sync, our bodies moving together at an almost frenzied pace. I close my eyes against the flood of sensations as the build-up of tension reaches its peak. My eyes fly open to watch Evan's face, his dark eyes and fierce expression almost enough to make me fall over the edge again.

We lie together in a heap, as we always do after finishing. Our kisses and touches are gentle now, slow and loving. When his breathing returns to normal and my heart no longer feels like it's trying to escape through my throat, we make a quick trip to the bathroom before dashing back to bed and into each other's arms.

As I'm drifting to sleep, it hits me that I was wrong about Evan proposing tonight. I guess his nerves were solely about executing his romantic plan and not about popping the question. I shift to peer at him and when I see his face is soft from sleep, I indulge in a moment of simply watching him. My heart swells with love, reminding me I don't need a ring on my finger, as long as I get to spend my life with this incredible man.

CHAPTER FIVE

❄

I'm startled awake by a string of sneezes.

"Ugh, sorry," Evan says, his voice muffled. I roll over to see him sitting up in bed clutching a wad of tissues to his face with one hand and holding a box of tissues in the other. His eyes are red-rimmed and watery.

"Oh no, that came on quick." I push into a sitting position and brush his cheek and forehead with the back of my hand. "No fever."

"It's not a cold. At least I don't think it is." He catches my hand as I move to drop it, pressing my palm against his cheek with a sigh. "It feels more like allergies."

When we first started talking about moving in together, I said we should get a cat. I'd always wanted one growing up, but my dad wasn't an animal person, and the apartment building where I lived after he died didn't allow pets. Evan told me he was allergic to cats, which I thought was a handy excuse and that he, like my dad, simply didn't want a pet. Then one night, Hugh and Ivy invited us to dinner at their place and Evan started sneezing the moment he walked in the door. Even when Ivy shut her sweet black cat Fiddlesticks away in their bedroom, Evan's eyes and nose continued to run. We finally had to go out to a restaurant, with a stop at the pharmacy for a pack of antihistamines first.

I stroke his cheek and his eyes slip closed. "I wonder what's setting you off. You were fine last night."

"My nose started itching when we got back here," he says. "I've never really been around horses, so I thought maybe my allergy extended to them. Doesn't explain why I'm like this twelve hours later, though."

"Do you want me to go get you some tea or something? Maybe bring you breakfast in bed?"

He gives me the barest hint of a smile. "Under other circumstances I'd say yes, but I feel like we'd have a bedroom full of Perrys within minutes. Jasper may seem standoffish, but you've never seen anyone go into mother hen mode faster than him."

I suppress a laugh at the image of Jasper clucking around Evan, taking his temperature, bringing him endless bowls of soup, and tucking him tightly into bed.

"Whatever you're picturing, multiply it by a thousand," Evan says, his smile growing as he studies my face. He coughs and reaches for the glass of water on the bedside table, but it's empty. I grab mine along with my birth control pill and take a quick sip before handing the glass to him.

Since we're planning to stay in today, I tell him he might as well keep his pajamas on and be comfortable. I'd like to stay in mine, but I caught Tucker staring at my chest the night we arrived when we were all sitting around talking in our pajamas. My breasts are small so I tend not to wear a bra if I don't need to, and I figured I'd be safe around Evan's family. The way Tucker was ogling me made me feel like he had x-ray vision and could see my bare breasts through the fleece of my pajama top. I'd prefer not to have a repeat today, so I get dressed while Evan lounges in bed for an extra few minutes.

"If family time becomes too much, I'll use my mystery malady as an excuse and we can escape to our bedroom, okay?" he says as we make our way downstairs. "We'll say I'm highly contagious so we need to be quarantined just th two of us. I'm sure Jasper will bring us our meals." He glances over his shoulder at me when I let out a little snort of laughter. His siblings come into view in the living room as we reach the bottom of the stairs, and the smile slips off his face. "What. The hell. Is that thing?"

I recognize Lina from her pictures: tall and slim with hair a few shades darker than the Perry men, worn in a long braid. She's holding court in the middle of the living room, cradling a giant ball of gray and white fur, and she startles at Evan's raised voice. "Oh, Evan, good morning. This is Mitzy." She lifts the bundle of fluff in her arms and kisses its head. "She's a purebred ragdoll cat. I called to tell you about her when I got her, don't you remember? Since none of the Perrys have been blessed with children yet, Mitzy is your first niece."

"I remember." Evan's voice borders on a low growl. "But I didn't expect you to bring Mitzy to Christmas since *I'm highly allergic to cats!*"

Lina's face goes blank. She looks from Evan to Mitzy and back again. "Oh. Yes. Right. I forgot."

When Evan opens his mouth, I grab his hand and squeeze it. I can practically hear the words about to spill from his lips—'*Of course you did, because you only ever think about yourself*—and I don't want this already bad start to escalate further. I release his hand and step forward, giving Lina what I hope is a warm smile. "Hi. I'm Gwen, Evan's girlfriend. It's so nice to finally meet you."

"Oh, yes, hello dear," Lina says absently, her attention on the squirming cat in her arms. "It's nice to meet you too. And allow me to introduce you—you too, Evan—to my man friend, Van." She wiggles her fingers toward the handsome Asian man standing a few feet away.

I just barely stop myself from laughing. For a second I thought she actually had a sense of humor and was joking about the 'man friend' thing, but her expression hasn't changed. *Okay then.* We exchange pleasantries, with Evan's being on the sullen side, not that I can blame him since his eyes and nose are practically streaming at this point.

"What are we going to do about Mitzy?" he asks.

"What exactly do you expect me to do? It's nearly a two-hour drive back to Toronto, and I can't simply leave her in my apartment all alone. Not only would she starve, she's a very social creature. Being alone for that length of time could do *untold* amounts of damage." She presses the cat closer to her chest and bounces her the way a mother would do with a fussy baby. "I suppose I can keep her in our bedroom for the next few days."

Evan turns away and sneezes into a tissue three times. When he straightens, he's out of breath and his whole face is red. "I woke up sneezing this morning and that's with us upstairs and you downstairs. Keeping her in your room won't make a difference."

"Well, we have quite the dilemma on our hands, don't we?" Lina says.

Evan's face grows to an alarming shade of red. Before he can say anything, Jasper steps in. "I'll run into town and pick up some antihistamines for you," he says. "I know it's not ideal, but..."

'Not ideal' is an understatement, considering antihistamines make Evan completely loopy. When he took them the night we went out for dinner with Hugh and Ivy, he was slurring his words and giggling at everything. Hugh had to drive us home and help me haul Evan into my apartment, where he flopped fully dressed into my bed and slept for the next ten hours.

Evan groans. "Okay, fine. Thank you, Jasper."

"Yes, thank you, Jasper." Lina wrinkles her nose and steps back when Evan sneezes again. I expect her to apologize for forgetting something as major as her brother's severe allergy, but she doesn't say anything else.

I guess Evan wasn't kidding about the chaos really starting once his older sister arrived.

❄ ❄ ❄

I hand Evan a cup of hot apple cider before setting my glass of eggnog on an end table and carefully squeezing into the armchair he claimed for us. "This is nice, isn't it? It's really starting to feel like Christmas."

True to his word, Jasper went to the pharmacy this morning and got Evan a supply of antihistamines. Despite asking the pharmacist for a brand that wouldn't make his brother drowsy, Evan's eyes have had a heavy-lidded, semi-stoned look to them all afternoon. At least it's been awhile since his last sneezing fit.

"Make sure to take lots of pictures since I won't remember anything from this Christmas." His upper lip curls, and I follow his gaze to see Malcolm and Sherée kissing in front of the fireplace. "Although maybe that's a blessing."

"Is everyone ready to decorate the tree?" Jasper asks, striding into the room carrying paper bags stamped with a logo I recognize from a fancy boutique in Toronto. He pulls the coffee table closer to the Christmas tree and removes several boxes of ornaments from the bags.

Soft Christmas music plays from the hidden stereo speakers across the room, and the air is scented with pine and spices. As he was preparing dinner, Jasper put a pot of mulled wine on the stove to simmer, along with the alcohol-free cider he picked up this morning since Evan can't mix booze and allergy meds. On my last trip to the kitchen to get Evan a refill, Malcolm was filling a punch bowl with eggnog and rum. I was going to stick to cider, but decided tree decorating with the Perrys called for hard alcohol.

Lina enters the room with a huff. "Poor Mitzy is *not* pleased about being kept in the bedroom. Van said since we'll be decorating the tree and that's a family activity, he'll stay in there with her."

"Gee, I'm so sorry my lifelong allergy has inconvenienced you, *Laurelina*," Evan says. "Maybe you should let her out of the room and see how long it takes me to asphyxiate."

I pause in my attempt to wriggle out of the armchair long enough to elbow Evan in the arm. He lets out a yelp and rubs at his bicep, scowling at me. I bite my tongue to keep from saying that if he's going to act like a baby, maybe he should go upstairs to bed. "Be nice," I whisper.

"My sister is trying to kill me," he hisses back, but his glassy eyes carry a spark that tells me he's trying not to laugh.

We gather around Jasper, who's now opening the boxes of ornaments. There are silver and blue balls, tiny off-white woodland creatures, silver ribbons, and several strings of clear lights. The decorations are simple and elegant, like something you'd find in a magazine or on TV.

"Where's the tinsel?" Evan asks.

"Oh, darling, tinsel is *so* passé," Lina says. I could be mistaken, but I think she just said that with a hint of a faux British accent. Now that I think about it, most of what she says sounds like Madonna during her Guy Ritchie years. "Has anyone even used it since the '90s?"

"Yes, *us*. Every single year. You know that, Lina. Mom loved tinsel, even though it was '*so passé*' and we've had at least a light sprinkling of it on the tree every year since they died. It was your turn to bring it this year."

"I think I can help," Hadley says, bounding into the room with a wooden keepsake box. She and Tucker disappeared upstairs about twenty minutes ago and I assumed they were taking a page from Malcolm and Sherée's book, except in private rather than out where everyone could see. She sets the box on one of the armchairs since there's no room left on the coffee table, and opens the lid.

"Oh man, I forgot about this stuff," Evan says.

"I did too until I got back from Europe and took all my things out of storage. This box was buried in a bigger box under a bunch of Mom's old blankets."

Over Evan's shoulder, I see the box is filled with colorful decorations, some of which look like they were made by children if the Popsicle sticks and streaky paint jobs are any indication.

"I'm pretty sure I saw a package of tinsel in here somewhere," Hadley continues. She looks up from the box, her eyes alight with pleasure. It's the most animated I've seen her since we got here.

I glance around at her siblings to see their reactions to the childhood treasures she brought. Malcolm has already moved forward to root through the box. Lina is studying the woodland creatures among Jasper's decorations, and Jasper...well, he looks like he just swallowed a lemon.

Hadley sighs. "What?"

"What? Nothing. I...it's just..." Jasper casts a longing glance at the ornaments spread out on the coffee table. "The tree in the lobby of the bank was so beautifully decorated this year, and it inspired me. The decorations we've used the last few years were dated and somewhat shabby. I bought these with an elegant, cohesive theme in mind, something you'd see...in one of those Hallmark movies you love so much!" He looks proud of himself for coming up with that last part. At Hadley's stormy expression, he quickly adds, "But we can certainly add some of these too. It's a big tree."

"That's settled then," Lina says before Hadley can even open her mouth to respond. "Let's use a light hand with the tinsel, though, yes? It makes a mess and if Mitzy were to get hold of any and swallow it, I fear it would have dire

61

consequences on her poor intestinal tract. She has quite the sensitive tummy as it is."

Jasper nominates Lina and me to put the lights on the tree while he finishes getting out the ornaments he bought. Evan and Hadley sit together on the couch going through the box of their childhood decorations. The way their heads are bent together as they talk and laugh fills me with warmth. Hopefully this will be the beginning of them finding their way back to each other and regaining their old closeness.

I haven't seen Tucker since dinner, but maybe he, like Van, decided tree decorating was more of a family event and decided to stay upstairs. And, of course, to the surprise of absolutely no one in this house, Malcolm and Sherée have gone back to making out in the corner.

The artificial tree from my childhood included built-in lights, so I've never had to string them myself. Lina informs me she usually gets stuck with light duty, so she takes the lead and shows me the easiest way. She's silent other than giving me directions. I feel like this small window of time together should be used to talk and get to know each other.

I rack my brain for a topic of conversation, finally landing on something I know will get her talking: herself. "Evan tells me you're working on your next novel?"

"That's right. Hard at work and moving swiftly along. It's due to the publisher in early spring and will hit shelves next autumn. It's strange because even though I published my best-selling, award-winning novel *Moonlight Over Silver Lake* months ago, those characters still take up so much of my heart and mind. Like now, for instance. This reminds me of a scene in the book when Kaitlyn and Fernando are decorating their first Christmas tree together. She thinks they should spray the tips of the branches with fake snow, and he thinks they should have colored lights instead of clear. That scene is a favorite among fans."

I have no clue how to respond to that. I don't want to admit I haven't read her book yet because I'm sure she'd take it as a personal affront. Despite meaning to, all of my reading lately has been limited to Bellevue Family Village press releases and social media posts. Ivy is a huge romance reader, though, and as soon as she found out Evan's sister had written a book, she read it and made sure the bookshop in the Village kept copies in stock.

"Oh! That reminds me!" Lina thrusts the string of lights into my arms and dashes from the room. I catch Evan's bewildered gaze and shrug.

Lina returns a few minutes later carrying a long, thin box. She reaches Malcolm and Sherée first and hands them each something from inside. Evan, Hadley, and Jasper are next on her way back to the tree. As she reaches me, I see the box holds dozens of small rectangular cards featuring her book cover, with a hole at the top just big enough for a silver ribbon to be looped through.

"They're tree ornaments," she says, hanging one front and center on the tree. "I mailed them to all the members of my fan club and had giveaways for them on social media. These are what's left, and I thought you might all appreciate having one, plus seeing some on our tree. They're all signed."

I turn my back on the rest of the room under the guise of continuing to put lights on the tree. I know if I look at any of the other Perry siblings' faces right now I'll likely burst into hysterical giggles. I don't have to see them to know there's a lot of eye rolling and head shaking happening right now.

When the lights are finally up—no thanks to Lina, who gets in my way hanging her book cover ornaments for the next five minutes—the others descend on the tree and begin hanging decorations. I notice Sherée hanging back around the coffee table, so I go stand with her.

"You okay?" I ask.

"Oh, yeah. I just like to let them have a few minutes to get started themselves," she says, running her fingers over the smooth faux fur of a fox ornament. "I think they let their differences keep them apart all year. They say they're busy and they *are*, but all of us except for you and Evan live in the Toronto area, and we hardly see each other. It's good for them to be together even if they don't know it."

I slide my phone from my pocket and snap a few pictures of the Perry siblings decorating the tree. Lina is talking about her book again and there's not even any eye rolling from the others.

The sweet bubble is burst a few minutes later when Hadley lets out a growl paired with a death glare aimed at her oldest brother. "Stop moving my decorations, Jasper! If you're going to keep rearranging them and hiding them at the back, I'll just put them away and we'll stick to your precious fancy theme."

As Jasper sputters out an apology and Lina jumps in with an anecdote about how her characters had to learn the art of compromise, Sherée and I exchange wry looks. I slip my phone back in my pocket; the photo-worthy family moments have come to an end.

"Do you have siblings?" I ask Sherée.

"Two sisters. The older one moved away and I haven't seen her in two years, which is fine by me. The younger one, well...we get along okay, but it's mostly for the sake of our parents. We have nothing in common other than shared blood and some fun childhood memories."

"And you don't spend Christmas with them?"

She shakes her head. "My parents were never big on the holidays. They did a bare bones Christmas for us growing up, and then when we all moved out they started going on cruises over the holidays. I've spent Christmases with friends over the years, though, and tensions tend to run high."

Hadley thrusts something into Jasper's hand and storms out of the room. Evan watches her go, his brows drawn together and his mouth pressed into a tight line. I expect him to go after her, but he turns back to the tree and hangs another ornament.

I wonder if it's common for families to bring out the worst in each other. Growing up, my friends were a mixed bag. Some of them hated their siblings, which I thought was typical rivalry, especially since a lot of them learned to get along better as they got older. Evan is normally the most easy going person I know, and yet when it comes to his family he's tense and often snarky. He's always told me how similar he and Hadley are in personality, so I doubt she's prone to tantrums, although that's what I'd call what just happened here.

As Sherée goes to join Malcolm, I ponder what she said about tensions running high around the holidays. It's supposed to be this wonderful, fun family time, yet I'm beginning to see my quiet Christmases with my dad were actually a blessing.

A few minutes later when Lina announces she's going to check on Mitzy, I seek out Evan so we can share an eye roll. If you can't beat 'em, join 'em, right? He's not by the tree or at the coffee table where the dwindling decorations are. I finally spot him sitting in one of the chairs by the fire, fast asleep. He's clutching an old-fashioned faded-red fire truck ornament in one hand. I take a sneaky picture of him—he's too cute not to—and then attempt to wake him so he can go lie down upstairs. I give his shoulder a gentle shake, and his head lolls back, followed by a soft snore.

I pry the ornament from his hand and go hang it on the tree. Jasper watches me, his eyes lingering on the fire truck. I assume he disapproves of how it clashes with his theme until I notice the downward turn of his mouth and the faraway look in his eyes.

I move into his line of sight and smile at him. I'm trying to think of something reassuring to say when his gaze darts away from mine and he ducks behind the tree.

So much for bonding with the Perry siblings today.

CHAPTER SIX

❄

Since everyone else is distracted and Evan will likely sleep for a while thanks to the antihistamines, I take the opportunity to make my escape upstairs. A bit of quiet time will do me good.

Soft voices inside Hadley's room make me unsure whether to pause or hurry by. As I approach her door, I realize the voices are coming from a movie rather than real people. I pause in the doorway and peek inside. Hadley is sitting up in bed with a laptop balanced on her lap. A thick blanket covers her legs and an open box of Candy Cane Viva Puffs sits beside her.

"Hey," she says, pausing her movie. "I don't suppose you came up here to hide out too?"

"As a matter of fact, I did." I take a small step into the room and she waves me forward, moving the cookies aside and patting the space beside her. It's a tight fit since it's a single bed, but I'm not about to turn her down when we've hardly had a chance to hang out the last couple of days. As soon as I'm sitting, she rearranges the blanket so it covers us both. The movie on the laptop is paused with Kate Winslet on the screen. "*The Holiday*! This is one of my favorite movies."

"Same here. I finished a Hallmark movie and started this one because I wanted something familiar and comforting. I can go back to the beginning if you want."

I study the screen; it's the part where Kate's character has just arrived in Los Angeles. "That's okay. For me, the movie really starts getting good when Cameron Diaz's character is debating leaving and Jude Law's character shows up, and that's next." She moves to unpause it, but I stop her. "Where's Tucker? I haven't seen him since dinner."

"He went to check out that saloon Evan mentioned," she says, avoiding my gaze. "I think a second afternoon of family games was too much for him and he needed a break." She points to the other bed, still not quite meeting my eyes. "Hey, do you want to shove the beds together? We'd probably be more comfortable not so squished into this one bed."

Each of us pushes a bed from one side until they meet in the middle, and then we make ourselves a comfy little nest of pillows and blankets. Even with twice as much room, we still end up sitting close together, the same blanket as before over our legs, and the laptop balanced on a pile of pillows in front of us.

Hadley hits play on the movie and puts the box of Viva Puffs between us to share. We watch in silence until the part where Arthur explains to Iris what a 'meet cute' is, and Hadley pauses the movie again.

"Will you tell me about yours and Evan's meet cute? He's told me bits and pieces, but I'd like to hear it from you."

"Of course." For some reason, I'm ridiculously touched by her request. She pushes the laptop aside and snuggles back against the pillows like a little girl getting ready for story time. "Evan and I have these mutual friends, Hugh and Ivy. They'd been telling us for ages how perfect we'd be for each other and how we should let them set us up, but neither of us was interested in a relationship. They invited me to their New Year's Eve party last year, and I assumed there was going to be a set-up, but they assured me Evan was out of town."

"And he was," Hadley says. "After our family Christmas he came back to Toronto with me for a few days because I was leaving for Europe the next week. We were supposed to spend New Year's Eve together, but there was this big storm in the forecast, so I sent him home, despite his protests."

"That's what he told us when he arrived unexpectedly at the party. He said since he was back in Bellevue, he might as well be with friends. This is going to sound so cheesy and cliché, but honestly, from the moment our eyes met there was this spark between us. When Hugh and Ivy introduced us, we hugged each other rather than shaking hands since it felt like we already knew each other."

I pause because I'm smiling so wide I can barely get the words out. "If you'd asked me a year ago if I believed in love at first sight, I would have laughed in your face. But that's what it was with your brother. We spent most of the party together and then ended up spending the night at Hugh and Ivy's place, with me on the couch and him on a pile of blankets on the floor nearby. From that day on, we were pretty much inseparable."

"That's so romantic." Hadley clutches her hands in front of her chest and closes her eyes briefly. "Love at first sight sounds ludicrous, but you guys are proof it happens. And here you are a year later, madly in love, living together, spending your first Christmas together. I'm gonna swoon."

I laugh. "I've done my fair share of swooning over the last year. Our relationship isn't perfect—there's no such thing—and we do drive each other batty at times, but he's the best thing that ever happened to me."

Hadley releases a gusty sigh and sits up to grab the second-last cookie. Her eyes cloud over as she bites into it.

"What about you? How did you and Tucker meet?"

"Oh, we knew each other in college," she says, waving her cookie-free hand. "We ended up living in the same building when I got back from Europe, and we started hanging out. Nothing nearly as romantic as you and Evan."

"There are different types of romance," I say slowly. She's eyeing the last cookie, so I prod the box in her direction. After a minute when she doesn't say anything else, I add, "Things must be serious if you invited him to spend Christmas with your family."

"Mm, yeah. He's great," she says around a mouthful of marshmallow.

Okaaay. This could be my only chance to learn anything real about Hadley, but she's not making it easy. I could change the subject or I could come right out and ask if something is going on with her that she'd like to talk about. The problem is, if I piss her off or alienate her, we still have a few days together in this house and it could make things awkward for everyone. I decide to tread lightly. "You guys seem so...mismatched?"

The quiet laugh she lets out sounds almost bitter, yet her voice is bright when she says, "You know what they say about opposites attracting." Her forced smile wobbles at the edges and she bites her lip.

"Hadley. Talk to me."

"I'm gay!" she blurts. Her wide eyes dart immediately to the door, where they linger for several seconds before shifting to me. "I'm gay. Or bi maybe, or—I'm not sure, I just know I'm not straight. Tucker is a friend. He didn't have anywhere to go for Christmas and I didn't want to come alone, so we agreed we'd pretend to be together."

I inch closer to her and reach tentatively for her hand. She grasps it and holds on tight. "Why didn't you want to come alone? What makes this year different?"

"I was in denial about being gay before. I've always been attracted to women, but thought...I don't know, I thought I'd grow out of it or something because I'd never actually *been* with a girl. But then when I went to Europe, I met this amazing woman and we fell in love. We traveled together for a few months until she had to go back to Australia. I was tempted to follow her, but..." She shrugs one shoulder and swipes at her eyes. "It wouldn't have worked. It was impossible to deny the truth anymore after that, though."

"And you don't want your family to know?" I try to keep my tone neutral so she doesn't think I'm judging her.

"I do? Maybe? But not now. I'm just coming to terms with it myself. I don't know how to add in their feelings and reactions too. In case you haven't noticed, the Perrys can be a lot." She gives me a wry smile.

"You know they'd still love you, right? Are you worried about that?"

"No." She tilts her head back and forth. "Not really. It's just that I'm the baby and I've always been different from the rest of them, except for Evan. I don't want them to see this as yet another thing that sets me apart. And I don't want them to treat me differently."

I cup my free hand around our joined ones as I mull over what to say. I've never had anyone come out to me like this before, and I know this is a monumental moment. I don't want to screw it up. "I obviously don't know your family well, but I do know Evan. I don't think the rest of your siblings would even think twice if you came out, but if for some reason they did, you'd still have Evan. And me." My throat tightens on the last few words as tears fill her eyes. "I would never pressure you to come out if you weren't ready, but I do wish you'd talk to your brother, even if it's not about that. He's been worried about you and he can feel the distance you've put between you two."

She frees her hand from mine so she can reach for the box of tissues on the nightstand. "I know, and I'm sorry for that. I'll talk to him, I promise." She wipes her eyes and blows her nose before pulling the laptop closer to us.

It's clear that's a sign she wants this conversation to be over, but I cover her hand before she can hit play again. "Thank you for trusting me enough to tell me."

"Thank you for listening," she says, staring straight ahead at the screen and blinking rapidly. She hits play when I release her hand, and we settle back into our lounging positions to watch the movie.

About an hour later, Evan stumbles past the door. Hadley pauses the movie and we wait to see if he'll come back, which he does. "Can anyone join this party?" he asks, slumping against the doorframe. His words are slurred, so I'm guessing he just took another dose of antihistamines and they're hitting him harder than they did earlier.

I pat the space beside me. He comes in and flops onto the bed, resting his head on my shoulder and throwing an arm across my stomach. "Jasper sent me upstairs to bed."

I smother a laugh as I catch Hadley's amused expression. "That was smart. You'll probably be more comfortable in bed than you were sitting in the chair."

"It wasn't because of that," he says slowly, pulling my hand toward him and playing with my fingers. "It was because I told off Lina."

Hadley sits up straighter, making a choked sound I think is a laugh. "You told her off? What'd you say?"

"I...don't really remember? I started sneezing again and I was wheezing a bit, so Jasper made me take another ant— anti*hisss*—pill—and Lina was going on and on about her book and her characters and blah blah fucking blah..." He trails off, making a talking motion with his hand. He stares at it and chuckles to himself, muttering about shadow puppets. "Anyway, I said something about her caring more about her fictional characters than anyone or anything else and Jasper got mad and sent me to my room."

I glance at Hadley again. Her eyes are wide and her lips are pressed together. She looks like she can't decide whether to laugh or cry as she gives me a helpless shrug.

Evan leans into my shoulder, peering around me at his sister. After a few seconds, his head drops back so he can meet my eyes. "Now both of my sisters hate me." His voice is a quiet, somewhat slurred murmur, yet I can tell from the way Hadley goes rigid next to me that she heard. Evan's eyes slip closed and his breathing evens within seconds.

The silence that follows is like a physical weight. I keep my eyes on Evan's face, afraid to look at Hadley. When I finally do, her forlorn expression almost makes me wish I hadn't.

She wipes the tears from her cheeks and gives me a resolute nod. "I promise I'll talk to him."

CHAPTER SEVEN

❄

Evan is still sound asleep the next morning when I wake up. He doesn't even stir when I shift to face him or roll away a few minutes later and get out of bed. After his rough day yesterday, I decide to let him sleep as long as he needs.

Tomorrow is Christmas Eve, which is the big celebration for the Perry family. It's when they do their traditional meal and each open one present. Evan explained Christmas Day is for lounging in pajamas, watching movies, and grazing on leftovers along with the junk food they get in their stockings.

Something feels off as I make my way downstairs. When my feet hit the last step, I realize how quiet it is. The last two mornings we've woken up to chattering voices and the clanking of dishes. I sniff the air and smell coffee and something cooking, but the kitchen is silent.

I peek around the corner to find Jasper sitting at the kitchen island, slumped over a cup of coffee. A plate with a fork on it sits off to the side. The kitchen is empty otherwise, and the usual breakfast buffet is missing, with just one small frying pan sitting on a back burner of the stove.

"Good morning," I say quietly, hoping not to startle him.

Jasper looks up from his coffee. "Good morning, Gwen. Did you sleep well?"

After Hadley and I finished watching *The Holiday*, we watched two more movies. By the time she helped me haul

Evan to bed—where he immediately started snoring so hard I thought he'd suck the curtains off the windows—Tucker still hadn't returned. I offered to stay up with Hadley, but finally gave in and went to bed around three. Jasper doesn't need to know all of that, though. "Fairly well, thanks. It's so much quieter here than in the city. Well, quiet except for your brother's drug-induced snoring."

I don't expect him to laugh since he rarely does, but I thought he might at least crack a smile. Instead he just nods and rises from his stool. "What can I make you for breakfast?"

"You don't have to make anything, Jasper," I tell him. "I can just have cereal or something."

"I don't mind, truly. I love to cook and I don't get to do it for anyone else the rest of the year."

Despite his neutral tone, there's something sad about his statement. I picture him rattling around his home in Toronto—I don't even know if he lives in a house or an apartment—making meals for one, keeping everything perfectly tidy and clean. Living in the same city as all but one of his siblings and yet rarely seeing them.

"An omelette would be nice," I say. "With cheese and mushrooms?"

"Coming right up." He pours me a cup of coffee and fixes it exactly how I like it. I don't remember telling him how I take my coffee, so he must have noticed on his own. The lump that formed in my throat the moment I found him alone in the kitchen grows.

"Where's everyone else?" I ask as he gets the eggs and cheese out of the fridge.

"Malcolm and Sherée are sleeping in. I assume Hadley and Tucker are too since he was out so late last night. I'm actually surprised to see *you* up so early." He pauses in his egg cracking to glance at me. He always seems to know what's going on, even when it's hard to fathom how he *could* know. "Lina and Van were up early and have already eaten. They're back in their room."

Now would be the perfect time for Jasper and I to do a little bonding. The problem is, I have no idea what to say. He runs so hot and cold, and his vibe is generally one of being closed off, like he's got walls around him with barbed wire and No Trespassing signs. I know he *can* relax because I enjoyed my time with him on our way to the Christmas tree farm. That seems to be an isolated incident, though.

Ultimately, I decide to keep my mouth shut rather than making idle chitchat. He sets a restaurant-worthy omelette and a slice of buttered toast in front of me a few minutes later, then tops up both our coffee cups.

"Did you ever think about becoming a chef?" I ask, cutting into the omelette and inhaling the delicious-smelling steam.

"I did contemplate it for a time," he says, reclaiming his stool, which is kitty-corner to mine. "I decided against it largely because of the cost of culinary school. It's also an incredibly demanding and high-stress job, and I don't think I'm cut out for that sort of environment. It's more a hobby of sorts, something I enjoy doing in my spare time with little pressure and pleasurable outcomes."

"Well, I'm glad we all get to benefit from your hobby while we're here," I tell him.

"Evan and I don't get to Toronto much, but I'm thinking we should change that in the new year. I'd like to take in a few shows and check out some of the exhibits at the Royal Ontario Museum. And more importantly, I think it'd be nice to visit you and the others sometimes. I can't believe Evan and I have been together for a year and this is my first time meeting everyone. Maybe we could make a regular trip to the city and you could cook for us."

I'm rambling. The curious way Jasper is looking at me makes me nervous, and the words keep spilling out. I wait several beats for him to respond, but other than a slow nod,

I get nothing. I shift my attention to my omelette, hoping he doesn't notice the blush I feel creeping into my cheeks.

It's strange to sit with someone who looks so much like Evan and yet is so different. I could see the obvious resemblance between Jasper and Evan immediately, but the more time I spend with Jasper, the more of his brother I see in him. I imagine he's what Evan will look like in a few years, with silvery threads creeping into his dark hair around the temples and sideburns. Evan already has more laugh lines than Jasper does, even though he's seven years younger. From what I've seen, I don't imagine Jasper's smiling muscles get much use, unlike Evan who's quick to laugh and smile.

I finish my breakfast in silence. The omelette started out delicious, but I can barely taste it by the time I'm done. I'd take a rowdy breakfast with everyone talking at once and Malcolm and Sherée sucking face in the corner any day over this awkward, heavy silence. I thank Jasper for breakfast and start to flee from the room when he says my name.

He's still sitting at the island, cradling his cup of coffee. "I appreciate you wanting to bring the family together more. It's a lovely idea and a well-meaning one, I know. But the distance between the Perry siblings is littered with years of misunderstandings, hurt feelings, and vast differences in personalities. You've seen how things are the last few days. We can barely get through a group activity without some mishap or other. Perhaps we're meant to stick to our once-a-year familial obligation at Christmas and be content with that."

I wonder if it's taken him all this time to formulate his response. His words seem as carefully chosen as always, delivered in a gentle tone, and yet to me they ring of 'mind your own business, you're not part of this family and don't know what you're talking about'. I'm tempted to tell him if he pulled the stick out of his ass and loosened his need to control and schedule everything, maybe things wouldn't be quite so tense, but there's no point. I simply nod and leave the room.

On my way to the stairs, a clatter draws my attention to the front hall. Upon investigation, I find Van donning his coat and scarf.

"You heading out?" I ask.

His head jerks in my direction. Unlike Jasper, he smiles when our eyes meet. "Going for a quick walk. It's such a nice day, I thought I'd take advantage of the fresh country air."

"Big change from Toronto, huh?"

"Oh yeah. It's not so bad in the winter, but in summer it's smog central." He pulls his gloves from the pocket of his coat with one hand and steps forward, extending the other hand to me. I'm confused for a second until I realize he wants to shake my hand. Hell, even then, I'm still confused. "It was so nice meeting you, Gwen. I wish I'd had time to get to know you and the others better. I hope you have a very happy Christmas."

He gives my hand a squeeze before releasing it and heading for the door. After he's stepped outside and closed the door, I stand rooted to the spot, stunned. I wonder how far he plans to walk that he's saying goodbye and wishing me a happy Christmas.

Despite Lina and I still being virtual strangers, my curiosity gets the best of me and I decide to seek her out. I dash past the kitchen, not wanting to see or speak to Jasper, and head down the hall where the downstairs bedrooms are. Giggles erupt from behind the closed bathroom door, and I recognize the laughter as Sherée's.

Having learned a sound like that is usually followed by an eyeful of something I'd rather not see, I pivot in the other direction, but it's too late. The bathroom door flies open and floral-scented steam spills out, along with

Malcolm and Sherée, both sporting dewy skin and skimpy towels.

"Morning," I say, averting my eyes.

"We've gotta stop meeting like this, Gwen," Sherée says, giving me a playful poke in the arm. I wave her off, but I'm chuckling now too. Their hushed voices trail down the hall, and when the bedroom door clicks shut, Sherée lets out a little shriek, followed by more giggling.

I carry on down the hall, freezing outside Lina's room when I hear Jasper's voice. He must have come this way when I was talking to Van. I take a step in the opposite direction and stop when I hear Lina say, "Evan wasn't wrong about everything last night, Jasper."

My ears perk up at the words. My dad always chastised me for being an eavesdropper when I was younger; it's something I've worked on over the years, but my curiosity often gets the better of me. Like now. When I *know* I should walk away and yet here I stand, head tilted toward the door to catch Lina's next words. *Sorry, Dad.*

"For example, he was right about me being an attention whore. And he didn't say it, because he couldn't have known, but I'm also a fraud."

"A fraud?"

"I can't seem to write," Lina says with a gusty sigh. "The words just won't come. I...is that a car running? Van isn't leaving, isn't he?"

"I'll go check." Jasper's voice is much closer than it was a moment ago. I flail around, unsure where to go so I don't get caught hovering outside the door listening to their private conversation. I can almost hear my dad laughing and saying 'I told you so, Gwendolyn' as I scramble to move away from the door. Jasper collides with me as he strides out of the room.

"Sorry!" I yelp as he grips my arms to steady me. The excuses my brain is churning up aren't needed because he simply gives a distracted nod, releases me, and carries on down the hall.

I wait a few beats. When Lina doesn't appear in the doorway to investigate, I peer into her bedroom. She's leaning over an open suitcase on the bed, eyeing the stack of clothes beside it. Mitzy is perched on one of the pillows at the head of the bed, sleeping.

"Are you leaving?" My voice comes out in a high squeak.

For a minute, I think she didn't hear me. She simply stands there, staring into the suitcase. She finally turns halfway toward me, forcing a smile onto her lips. "*I'm* not, no. Van is. We've decided to part ways. He'll be returning to Toronto today and taking Mitzy with him so Evan can enjoy the rest of Christmas without being high on allergy meds."

Before I have a chance to respond, she shifts back toward the bed and begins placing items into the suitcase. "A breakup is good fodder for fiction, you know. Lived experiences always make writing more realistic. I'll take this heartache and channel it into my next book."

I'd like to think this is her pain talking, but considering everything comes back to her and her writing, I find it hard not to roll my eyes. I don't know her well enough to intuit what to offer right now—a shoulder to lean on? A change in topic? A reassuring word? A pithy reminder there are more fish in the sea? My friends always sat with me and let me wallow or rage over breakups, all while providing endless hugs, chocolate, and alcohol.

"Would you have been upset if I left?" Lina asks.

"Oh. I..." What do I say? I hardly know her. Our conversations have been centered on her and her writing. She hasn't asked me a single thing about myself or made any effort to get to know me. "Evan would be disappointed. Especially if he thought he'd driven you away. He told me last night he said some things he regrets."

She nods slowly. "Does he, though? Regret them, I mean."

Honestly? I doubt it. I don't know what he said, but it seems like it was a long time coming. "You'd have to talk to him about that. I'm sure he'll want to talk to you anyway when he wakes up. Hopefully he'll be in a better mood once he's not sneezing his head off." I keep my tone light, hoping to draw a smile from her. She just presses her lips together and nods again. "Okay, well. I'll see you later, I guess."

As I step out of the room, she says, "I know you were standing in the hallway when I was talking to Jasper."

My cheeks flame. *Busted.* "I'm sorry, I know that was incredibly rude."

She lifts one shoulder. "If it's rude then we'll be rude together. I get some of my best ideas by eavesdropping on people's conversations."

I choke out a laugh. "Good to know. Maybe I should become a writer too."

"Maybe you should. I hope you have an easier time getting words out than I do."

"I heard you telling Jasper you can't write? I thought you said your next book was coming along nicely."

Lina shoves the suitcase aside and plops onto the bed, startling the cat out of slumber. She makes a quiet clicking noise until Mitzy moves closer, and she gathers the cat into her arms, cradling her like a baby. Mitzy's purr is so loud it sounds like a small engine.

"When I wrote *Moonlight Over Silver Lake*, it was mostly on a whim. I'd dabbled in creative writing through high school and college, but never thought of doing it professionally. The characters came to me out of the blue one night, and when I sat down to write, the words poured out of me. I let a few friends read it, and they loved it. That was all it took for me to decide to publish it. I thought a few people might read it, if I was lucky. I never dreamed of it achieving the success it has. But...I think my head grew along with the success of the book."

She's kept her gaze on Mitzy this whole time, as if relating her story to the cat is easier than telling me directly. She looks at me now, though, and I'm surprised to see the small self-deprecating smile curving her lips.

"I've always liked attention. My mother used to joke that I came out of the womb ready for the spotlight." She smiles sadly, returning her attention to Mitzy. "As the number of reviews and members in my fan club swelled, I craved more. It was never enough. It is never enough. But now I've let it all go to my head and I can't write. I'll be a one-hit wonder, shining brightly for a time before quickly being forgotten."

"Why did you say you were working hard on your next book then?"

"Because that's what people want to hear." She looks at me again and adds quickly, "Not you. I know I could have—*should* have—confessed the truth to you or my siblings. I find I'm having trouble separating my public persona from my personal one. My fans want to talk about *Moonlight* and they want to know how the next book is coming. I'm grateful to them, and yet they want so much from me. Somewhere along the way, I left the public persona switch on and I'm not sure how to turn it off."

I've been keeping my distance, standing just inside the doorway. Part of me is afraid Lina will suddenly realize she's pouring her heart out to me and she'll clam up. I think my interaction with Jasper at breakfast has put me a bit off kilter, made me doubt myself and my place among the Perrys. I may not be an official part of this family, but I love Evan more than anything, and his siblings' happiness affects him too, which in turn affects me.

So I cross the room and sit on the foot of the bed, leaving several feet of space between us. "Now would be a good time to try. Your family loves you and they're a safe space." I pause as the irony of this conversation hits me. I basically told the same thing to Hadley mere hours ago. I never would have expected to have the Perry women confess their deepest secrets to me of all people over Christmas vacation. Sometimes it's easier to spill your guts to someone you don't know well, though. Having been in therapy, I can attest to how true that is.

"You don't have to be *'on'* with them," I add. "They don't expect Laurelina Peregrine to show up for tree decorating or movie night. They want Lina Perry, their sister."

With a sigh, she lifts her head and finally maintains eye contact with me. Her gaze is piercing as it searches mine. "My little brother is quite lucky to have met someone like you. You're a welcome addition to this family, Gwen."

Wow. "Thank you," I say, swallowing past the tightness in my throat.

She clears her own throat and straightens, her eyes dipping back down to Mitzy. Our warm, fuzzy moment is gone as quickly as it came. You can't have everything, I guess. I conjure up an image of Evan's index cards with details about his siblings, and picture the line on Lina's that read 'allergic to expressions of emotion'. I'd thought it was an exaggeration, especially since she writes romance novels, but he wasn't kidding.

"I'll let you get back to packing for Van," I say, rising from the bed. "I may not be a writer, but I *am* a good listener, so if you ever want to talk or bounce ideas off me, I'm here."

Her eyebrows disappear under her dark bangs. "You know, I just might take you up on that. Oh, and you're in PR, aren't you?" At my nod, she says, "Maybe we could go over my social media together at some point. I have a personal assistant who handles most of my promotional posts, but I think I should consider shaking things up in the new year. More Lina and less Laurelina, perhaps."

"I'd be happy to help. We'll find some time before we all head home in a few days." I don't mention that I checked out her social media feeds months ago. It was so impersonal and promo-heavy I assumed it was run by a PR person. Or a robot. I make my way to the door, telling her I'll see her later.

"Oh, and Gwen? Be sure to tell Evan that his cat-niece Mitzy says goodbye." Her expression remains placid, but her eyes gleam with amusement.

Did Lina Perry just make a joke? I'll consider that a Christmas miracle.

CHAPTER EIGHT

❄

The last twelve hours have been an emotional roller coaster. Growing up, I often entertained the idea of becoming a psychologist, but ultimately decided against it. My conversations with the Perry sisters—and attempting to understand Jasper—have left me wondering if I missed my calling in life.

I sneak into the bedroom I'm sharing with Evan, hoping he's still asleep and I can crawl into bed with him. I'm not sure what The Plan is for today—because you can be sure Jasper has one—but I could already use a nap.

It's not meant to be, though. Evan is sitting up in bed, eyes glued to his phone. A pile of discarded tissues litters the bedspread around him, and his nose is Rudolph red.

"Morning," he says, his voice rough from disuse. "Thanks for letting me sleep. I hope my family didn't pounce on you."

I crawl into bed beside him. I want to snuggle, but the thought of being sneezed on keeps me on my side of the bed. "It was actually quiet downstairs. Jasper made me breakfast, and everyone else was doing their own thing." I don't tell him about Lina sending Mitzy home with Van in case she changes her mind.

Evan aims his phone screen in my direction and points to the movie listing there. "There's a special showing of *The Santa Clause 2* in town tonight. We could go early and check out some of the shops that were closed last time, have dinner, and then go to the movie?"

Now I do snuggle against him—watery eyes and red nose be damned. "That sounds perfect."

We stay in bed until Evan's stomach starts growling. Other than a commotion down the hall a while ago, the house has been silent. Maybe everyone else is tapped out on family time already too.

Downstairs, we find Hadley standing in front of the tree with her back to us. When she reaches up to lightly touch one of the ornaments, I realize the tree looks a lot different than it did last night when I snuck out of the room. The decorations from the Perry siblings' childhood are no longer tucked away on low branches or at the back of the tree; they're mixed in prominently with Jasper's fancy color-coordinated ornaments. There's even a light sprinkling of tinsel across the branches.

"It looks beautiful," I say. Hadley whips around, swiping at her wet cheeks. Her quick smile tells me she'd prefer if I glossed over the obvious fact she's been crying. "Did you do a little switcheroo while Jasper wasn't looking?"

"It was like this when I came down just now. They must have done it last night after we went upstairs." She points to the mantel, where several faded trinkets I recognize from Hadley's box sit among the framed family photos. Evan goes over to the fireplace for a closer look.

I inch closer to Hadley and whisper, "Are you okay? After last night?"

She tilts her head back and forth. "Yes and no." She loops her arm around my waist and directs me toward the armchair I've claimed as my favorite, the one that's big enough for Evan and me to squish into together. "I've asked Jasper to round up the others."

Before I can ask why, Malcolm and Sherée enter the room, followed by Lina and Jasper. Hadley asks everyone to take a seat as she moves to stand in front of the Christmas tree.

"I'm having major déjà vu right now," Evan says, wriggling into place beside me. To the room at large, he adds, "Remember those Christmas pageants we used to put on every year for Mom and Dad? We'd get dressed up and sing songs, do little plays we made up. When Hadley was old enough, she was always the one who introduced each act. Are you about to put on a show for us, Hads?"

Hadley gives a wobbly smile, her throat bobbing as if she's swallowing down a lump of emotion. "Something like that." She wrings her hands as everyone else gets settled, then clasps them in front of her, her tight grip turning her knuckles white. "I wanted everyone together so I'd only have to say this once. Tucker and I broke up this morning and he left for Toronto about fifteen minutes ago. He asked me to say his goodbyes and thank-yous for a nice time over the last few days."

"Oh, the Perry women are unlucky in love, aren't we?" Lina says, her tone wistful. "Van and I broke up this morning too. He's headed back to Toronto as well, along with my precious Mitzy. We—well, never mind, this isn't about me. Sorry, darling, carry on."

I never thought I'd hear the words 'this isn't about me' coming from Lina's mouth.

"Are you okay?" Evan asks Hadley.

"Yeah. Or at least I will be. Tucker and I really weren't all that compatible..." She trails off and spins on her heel to face the mantle, raking her hands through her dark hair. After a minute of staring at the family photos there, she pivots back to face the room, her expression determined. Her eyes lock on mine, and I give her a small nod of encouragement.

She takes a deep breath through her nose and lets it out slowly through her mouth. "That's not all I want to tell you, though. I w-wanted to tell you...I thought you should all know..." Blowing out an exasperated sigh, she crosses her arms over her chest, then immediately lets them fall back to her sides. "I'm gay."

Her words are met with silence. It's so quiet in here I can hear the fridge humming in the kitchen. Hadley's eyes go wide, panicked. Just as I attempt to free myself from the chair, everyone else moves at once, jumping up from their seats and crowding around Hadley. Jasper is the first to reach her and he wraps his arms around her, his usual stiffness gone. The way he holds her and murmurs softly into her ear makes my eyes fill with tears. I can't hear what he's saying, but it must be the right thing because Hadley smiles and closes her eyes, tears slipping down her cheeks.

Malcolm and Sherée embrace her next, going for a group hug and telling her they love her no matter what and they're glad she told us. Sherée tells her she knows some people in Toronto she can set her up with in the new year if she's interested. Hadley's cheeks turn pink as she laughs, shrugs, and says, "Maybe. We'll see."

"In my novel, *Moonlight Over Silver Lake*, the main character's best friend Trina is gay, you know," Lina says, giving Hadley a quick hug, then holding her at arm's length. At Hadley's indulgent smile, Lina quickly adds, "But this is real life, of course. I hope you know you can tell us anything, anytime." She kisses Hadley's cheek and releases her.

Evan steps up when Lina moves away. He and Hadley simply look at each other for several long moments, a silent conversation seeming to pass between them. Finally, he wraps his arms around her and she buries her face in his neck.

"I love you no matter what, you know that, right?" Evan says, his voice wavering. "All I want is for you to be happy."

I step back to give them some privacy as they whisper to each other. I'm relieved when Sherée waves me over to join her and Malcolm by the fireplace. She doesn't say anything, she just smiles and slings her arm around my shoulder. I'm touched by the gesture and grateful for the contact. Jasper says he's going to get lunch started, and Hadley gives Evan a final squeeze before following her oldest brother into the kitchen.

"We'll see you at lunch," Sherée says, patting my arm before taking Malcolm's hand and pulling him away. Lina disappeared a few minutes ago, so now it's just Evan and me. He crosses the room and walks straight into my open arms.

"You knew, didn't you?" he asks.

"She told me last night when we were alone. I wanted to tell you, but she told me in confidence, and I couldn't break her trust."

Evan releases me and leans one elbow on the mantle, resting his head in his hand and massaging his temple. When he looks at me, his expression morphs to one of concern and he reaches for my hands, holding them tightly. "I'm not upset that you knew. Or that my sister is gay, if that's what you're thinking." I shake my head quickly to assuage his worries. "I'm just sort of in shock, I guess? I have all these thoughts swirling through my head. Hadley and I have always been the closest out of all our siblings. Was she afraid to tell me? Did she think I'd react badly? Is this why she's been acting so weird since she got back from Europe? And yet I feel like a selfish prick for wondering all these things because I know this isn't about me, and I want to do whatever I can to support her."

"You're allowed to feel however you feel," I tell him, raising our joined hands and pressing them against my chest. "It's a lot to take in. I think you guys need some time on your own to talk."

"Yeah, but when?"

I think about the plans for the next few days. Surely at some point tomorrow or on Christmas Day they can steal at least a few minutes alone. I could lock them in a room together and guard the door to make sure no one disturbs them. Or… "You could take Hadley with you today instead of me. You could wander the town, have dinner, then see the movie together. She told me last night *The Santa Clause 2* was the first movie you two saw together after your parents died."

The smile that curves his lips is wistful. "It was. It felt like the first time either of us had laughed in months." He's silent for a few moments, lost in thought. "You love that movie too, though. Maybe the three of us could go together."

I shake my head before he even finishes speaking. "No, it would be better just the two of you. You haven't had more than five minutes alone since last Christmas and you need this."

He releases my hands so he can grip my hips and pull me closer, closing the already-small distance between us. He presses his lips to mine once, twice. He lingers on the third kiss, letting his tongue sweep out for the briefest taste. "You're amazing. Have I told you lately that I love you?"

"Yes, but I never get tired of hearing it. Tell me some more. And feel free to go into detail."

He tells me over and over that he loves me while peppering my entire face in kisses. We're a mass of giggles and swollen lips by the time Jasper interrupts to tell us lunch is ready.

"Let's go tell your sister she gets to escape the madhouse with you for the evening," I say, giving Evan one last kiss and pulling him toward the kitchen.

❄ ❄ ❄

Malcolm and Sherée decide to go on a date too, so they carpool into town with Evan and Hadley. I bundle up and go for a long walk down our quiet street and around the property of the rental house, sucking in huge lungfuls of fresh, wintry air, and pausing occasionally to make itty bitty snowmen. When I return inside, I make myself a snack before escaping upstairs, where I watch movies on Hadley's laptop and text with Ivy and a few other friends.

Around the time I think Jasper will be making dinner, I go downstairs and find Lina in the kitchen instead. "Looks like it's just you and me for dinner," she says, clapping her oven-mitt-clad hands together. "Jasper went out, but being Jasper, he made us a casserole to pop in the oven. It'll be ready in a few minutes. Shall we open some wine?"

"Absolutely." I don't ask where Jasper is. Maybe he needed a break from all the family togetherness too and decided tonight would be a good night since half the family was out anyway.

I'm surprised to find myself enjoying Lina's company at dinner. She asks about Evan's and my life in Bellevue and my job at the Village. I ask her about her writing, and despite being hesitant to talk about it at first, I assure her I want to know. She happily tells me all the details I suspect no one else will listen to, at least not without rolling their eyes.

We've made it through a bottle and a half of wine by the time we finish dinner and clean up. She tells me she's going to her room to see if she can fill a blank screen with words, and I wish her luck. She starts from the room and then doubles back to give me a quick, slightly stiff hug.

Feeling pleasantly warm and satiated, I head for the living room. I get a fire going in the fireplace and turn on all the Christmas lights while leaving the main lights off. I spend a few minutes simply standing in the middle of the room enjoying the glow before flopping onto the couch closest to the window. My delight escalates when I see giant flakes of snow fluttering from the sky and collecting on top of the thin layer of sparkling white on the ground.

My happy little bubble wavers slightly when I hear the front door open and shut a while later. It's too early for the foursome to be back, and they wouldn't enter silently anyway, which means it can only be Jasper. I curl further into the couch, hoping to make myself invisible.

"Beautiful evening."

So much for that. In the reflection from the window, I see Jasper standing in the doorway.

He clears his throat and steps further into the room. "I fear I hurt your feelings this morning. That wasn't my intention."

"Oh. That's okay, Jasper." It's *not* okay, but Evan was right the other day when he said to pick your battles when it comes to his siblings. If I'm going to survive Christmas with the Perrys, I need to remember not only to pick my battles, but also the fact the Perry siblings are very different people.

Despite Evan's warnings about Jasper and Lina being standoffish, part of me expected it wouldn't be so bad or maybe I'd be able to win them over. Evan is so open about his feelings and he's not afraid to dig deep and even shed a few tears. He's never once made me doubt how he feels about me, and when we disagree or argue, he's always the one doing the encouraging to talk things out. Those traits must have skipped Jasper and Lina, and Evan got an extra heaping of compassion and empathy in his DNA.

"As you may have noticed, I'm a bit...socially awkward," Jasper says. "I often find it hard to relate to people, and I tend to say the wrong thing. I know my siblings love me, but I don't think they like me very much."

I sit up straighter and shift my body to face Jasper. His tone is matter-of-fact, the way it always is. He's not seeking pity or probably even sympathy, but my heart aches at his words. "Will you come sit with me?"

"You were enjoying the peace and quiet, though. I should leave you be."

He really wasn't kidding about the socially awkward thing. I change tactics and say firmly, "Jasper. Come sit with me."

He crosses the room silently and sits on the opposite end of the couch. His posture is so rigid it makes my back hurt just looking at him. Even with only the two of us sitting here in the dark, quiet living room, he can't let himself relax.

"Did you know I was living on the west coast when my parents died?"

I'm so taken aback by the seemingly random question, it takes me a minute to answer. "No, I didn't know that. I guess I assumed you were still in Bellevue or maybe Toronto."

He shakes his head slowly. "I fell in love with a wonderful woman in university and moved with her to Vancouver after we graduated. We had been split up for a few months when my parents died, which made it easier to return to Bellevue to care for Evan and Hadley. I loved Vancouver, but I moved there mostly for her, and the whole city reminded me of her. Reminded me that the one impulsive thing I'd ever done in my life had ended in heartache."

"I'm sorry, Jasper."

He lifts one shoulder. "It is what it is. I would have come back regardless because Evan and Hadley needed me. Lina and Malcolm were both still in university. Neither of them were in a place to put their lives on hold and suddenly become guardian to two grieving teenagers."

Evan has talked a lot about those years with Jasper. He was sixteen and Hadley was fifteen when their parents died. He stayed for a year after he turned eighteen so Hadley wouldn't be on her own with Jasper, and then they all went their separate ways. He told me once that as an adult he can appreciate everything his brother did for them, even though as a teenager all he saw was how strict Jasper was, how he created schedules for them, enforced a ridiculous curfew, made them keep up their grades and get involved in so many extracurriculars they hardly had any free time.

I've never thought of it from Jasper's perspective, likely because I never met him before this week. He could have let his siblings go into foster care—it wouldn't have been for long—or live with the reclusive great aunt Evan told me about. Instead, he gave up his whole life and moved across the country so his younger siblings wouldn't be split up or sent away. My heart always broke at the thought of sixteen-year-old Evan losing his parents and being stuck with his strict older brother, but it must have been scary for Jasper too. Lonely and isolating. That kind of sacrifice speaks to a lot of emotional depth, even if he has trouble showing it.

"I'd like to be closer to them now," he says. "I'd like to have a friendly relationship, one where they don't simply tolerate me. I know much of that begins with me and trying to...loosen up." The way he says it almost makes me laugh. It sounds like he's talking about a completely foreign concept, which I guess he is. "My youngest brother met the love of his life and I didn't meet her for almost a year. My baby sister was hiding a huge secret about herself and didn't feel comfortable confiding in us. In *me*. It makes me feel like I've failed somehow."

I inch closer to Jasper. His eyes go wide as if I'm a wild animal about to pounce. I want so badly to reach out and take his hand, but I don't think we're quite there yet.

"I've always wanted what's best for the people I love," he says after a minute, staring past me at the softly falling snow outside. "I'm the oldest, it was my duty to step in and keep our family together. It only occurred to me in the last year or two that I was so busy worrying about Evan and Hadley and trying to do right by them that I didn't let myself grieve our parents properly. I somehow compartmentalized and separated the fact I was an adult and Evan and Hadley were still children, at least in the eyes of the law, and all I could see was how they lost their parents. I'd made it to adulthood and had moved out, but they were still living at home, still needed our parents in many ways. So I did my best to fill that role, even though in hindsight I see I took it too seriously."

"Not everyone would do what you did, you know. Even if you did maybe take it too seriously, Evan and Hadley are both successful, well-adjusted people. Don't underestimate your role in that."

Jasper pats my hand where it lies between us on the couch before getting to his feet. I half expect him to leave, but he crosses the room to stand in front of the tree, folding his arms over his chest.

"If I didn't completely scare you off during our conversation this morning—or our conversation now—I'd like to take you up on your idea of coming to Toronto to visit. We could do family dinners, get everyone together. Start small, maybe once every few months, and work our way up. You and Evan are welcome to stay in my spare bedroom when you come."

I get to my feet and join him in front of the tree. "I'd love that. And you could come visit us in Bellevue. Most of our friends live in town, so we haven't had anyone christen our spare room yet." I step closer to him, closing the distance between us. There's that wide-eyed look again. "I'm going to hug you now. Is that okay?"

"Oh. Well. I guess that would be all right."

Okay, so we still have some work to do. One of my goals will be working up to natural hugging instead of having him respond as if I asked him if I could give him a root canal. I wrap my arms around his shoulders and he puts his arms tentatively around my waist. It's like hugging a mannequin, but at least he gives me a gentle pat on the back as he pulls away.

"We're officially friends now, you know that, right?" I say, moving back to give him some space. "And just so you know, I'm the type of person who would do anything for her friends."

"Friends." Another seemingly foreign concept to Jasper. I push away the sadness that thought brings and allow pleasure and pride to take its place. I never would have thought I'd make this kind of progress with Jasper. This feels monumental. "Yes. Friends. I quite like that idea."

❄ ❄ ❄

Jasper escapes to his room and I return to the couch to enjoy the beautiful view. The glowing tree, crackling fire, and falling snow combine to make the perfect peaceful evening. When Evan told me we'd be spending Christmas in a rented house in the country, I imagined hot chocolate by the fire, playing in the snow, and stolen kisses between activities with his family. Despite his warnings not to expect much alone time or peace, I didn't anticipate dodging a horny couple at every turn, sticking to Jasper's rigid schedule, or being present for not one but two breakups.

But I also didn't expect to feel so much for the Perrys so soon. They may all have different ways of expressing themselves, and some of them may be allergic to displays of emotion and affection, but they've each welcomed me in their own way and made me feel like I belong. There must be something about the Perrys; I fell for Evan fast and hard, and now I'm doing the same with his entire family.

The sound of car doors closing draws me from my thoughts. Quiet voices and laughter fill the front hall a few minutes later. Malcolm and Sherée are the first to appear; they don't notice me sitting here as they pass by on the way to their bedroom. Evan and Hadley amble into the living room, arms slung around each other's waists and heads bent close as he says something that makes her laugh.

She's the first to spot me. She releases Evan and hands him one of the two takeout containers she's holding. "Thank you for letting me go in your place tonight, Gwen. It was exactly what we needed. I'm going to go get in the tub and let you two have some much-needed alone time." She kisses her brother's cheek before blowing me a kiss and disappearing up the stairs.

Evan admires the tree and the fireplace on his way to the couch. He kisses me the moment he sits down—his lips taste like popcorn and root beer. I kiss him again, inhaling the crisp scent of snow and peppermint surrounding him.

"You had fun tonight?" I ask.

"So much fun. It was like old times, back when it was the two of us against the world, you know? We were so caught up in talking we almost missed the movie." He hands me the takeout container Hadley gave him. "These are for you, from that bakery in town."

I open the lid and nearly squee when I see the assortment of Christmas goodies inside. I immediately pop one of the tiny mince tarts into my mouth. This night keeps getting better.

"Hadley wanted me to tell you she already loves you and can't wait to get to know you better. She wants us to come visit her in Toronto in the new year, and I told her she should come stay with us sometime."

"Something to look forward to through the seemingly endless Ontario winter." I rifle through the box and pick out a miniature pale blue macaron decorated with sparkly white icing in the shape of a snowflake.

Evan leans in closer, grinning as I make happy little eating noises. "She asked me why we weren't engaged yet."

I nearly choke on my cookie. "She *did*?"

He chuckles, brushing away the crumbs that flew from my mouth when I spoke. "She did. She said we're obviously meant for each other and we're madly in love, so what am I waiting for?"

I shove yet another macaron into my mouth—they *are* mini after all—to buy myself time to mull over my thoughts. Evan takes my hand, lacing our fingers together. I meet his soft, searching eyes. "The other day when you were planning your big surprise and acting all twitchy, I thought it was because you were going to propose."

I expect surprise at my admission, but he tilts his head and nods once. "I actually considered it. I've thought about it so many times over the last few months."

My heart swells at his words. "What's stopped you?"

"These past few months have been a whirlwind of moving in together and both of us getting busier at work. I guess part of me figured we're already committed to each other and living together, so there's no real rush. Before we came here, I decided if everything went well over Christmas and you didn't run screaming after a week with my family, I'd bring it up when we got home and both had time off with no distractions."

"I'm still here. No running for the hills, now or ever. This time with your family has made me an honorary Perry."

"Well, I'd like to make you an *official* Perry."

"Are you asking me to marry you, Evan?" My voice is high and wobbly from the excited laughter I'm keeping at bay.

He squeezes my hands and brings them up to his mouth, brushing his lips over one, then the other. He meets my gaze over our joined hands and says, "Marry me, Gwendolyn. I don't have a ring. I know it's not exactly romantic, but I was thinking we could pick out your ring together in the new year. You'll be wearing it for the rest of your life so I want you to be happy with it."

Oh god. I've done such a good job of keeping the floodgates in check until now. "In my opinion, that's the very definition of romantic."

His eyes glitter, reflecting the lights from the Christmas tree across the room. "So is that a yes?"

"It's a *hell* yes. Nothing would make me happier than being your wife." I set the takeout box on the end table beside the couch and practically launch myself at him. We both laugh as he falls back on the couch with me on top of him, and we're still laughing as our lips meet. The humor fades when our tongues touch and intertwine. He grips my hips and shifts me higher, creating delicious friction between our bodies. I grind against him, eliciting moans from both of us. His hand slips under my shirt, skating over my stomach and leaving goosebumps in its wake. Just before he cups my breast, I pull away and clamp my hand over his.

"Wait." I'm so breathless you'd think I'd just run up and down the stairs a dozen times. "I think one pair of exhibitionists in the Perry family is more than enough. Let's leave that to Malcolm and Sherée and take this upstairs to the privacy of our bedroom."

Evan groans, shifting me so I'm no longer pressing against his erection.

"I'll make it worth your while," I whisper in his ear, giving him a little nip. "We've had a lot of sex in the past year, but something tells me we're *really* going to enjoy just-got-engaged sex." I push myself off the couch and reach for his hand, laughing at his intrigued expression. "I'm pretty sure it's after midnight by now, which means it's Christmas Eve. Come let me jingle your bells."

He grabs my hand and jumps off the couch, sweeping me into his arms. Laughter vibrates through his chest and into mine. "Life will never be boring with you by my side, Gwen, that's for sure."

CHAPTER NINE

❄

The mood the next morning is much more relaxed than it has been any other morning so far. Jasper is in his element once more preparing a feast for breakfast, and we all crowd around the kitchen table to enjoy it. Lina and Hadley are more at ease than I've seen them yet. Neither of them seems worse for wear over their breakups, although Lina has mentioned how much she misses Mitzy already. Thankfully she was out of earshot of Evan at the time.

After breakfast, Hadley invites all the women to join her in making cookies and makes everyone else clear out of the kitchen.

"But there are plenty of baked goods. And I really should start on the dinner prep," Jasper says, eyeing the fridge where the giant turkey is waiting to be...well, whatever you do to a giant turkey to get it ready for Christmas dinner.

Hadley shakes her head and gives her oldest brother a gentle shove toward the doorway. "You'll have plenty of time to cook dinner, I promise. I think it's time to start a new tradition, and I want it to be for the women in this family to make cookies at Christmas."

"Isn't that kind of sexist?" Malcolm asks.

"Do you want to bake cookies with us, Mal?" she asks, her voice sugary sweet.

"No," he grumbles.

Hadley asks her other two brothers, who both decline. "There you have it. Not sexist, I just know you all too well."

"Be sure to tidy up after yourselves, please," Jasper says over his shoulder as his brothers lead him from the room. "And you can leave the oven on when you're done so it'll be ready to put the turkey in."

Hadley begins pulling ingredients from the fridge and cupboards while directing the rest of us to get everything else we'll need. She has Sherée pull up some Christmas music on her phone, and soon the four of us are measuring and mixing. The room is full of our chatter and laughter mixed with the scents of cinnamon, orange, and chocolate. I have a feeling I'll associate these smells with a Perry Christmas from now on.

When the timer goes off for the first batch of cookies, we all gather around like proud parents as Sherée dons oven mitts and removes the tray from the oven.

"Well, crap," Hadley says.

Lina holds up a finger hesitantly. "That would be my fault. It said to space them two inches apart, but I didn't think it would matter."

We all look at the cookies, which are basically big blobs stuck together in pairs.

"They look like eyes," Lina says, tilting her head and examining the cookies. "Anyone good with a piping bag? We could do something with icing to make them look more like eyes and say we meant to have them look that way."

"Oh!" Sherée signals for us to wait as she dashes from the room. She returns a minute later with a bag of Hershey's Kisses. She unwraps two and places them strategically on a set of stuck-together cookies.

"See?" Lina says. "Eyes."

Hadley snickers. "I don't think that's what Sherée was going for." I peer over her shoulder and see the eyes have become... well, boobs. "Do you ever *not* have sex on the brain?"

"Honey, I'm married to your brother, of course I have sex on the brain."

Hadley makes a disgusted face that brings out her resemblance to Evan. "Gross," she mutters, but her eyes dance with mirth.

As we get the next batch ready, Lina leaves the kitchen and returns with a small notepad and pen. She sits at the kitchen table and scribbles in the notebook, completely oblivious to Hadley and Sherée, who are singing "Rockin' Around the Christmas Tree" at the top of their lungs. When she closes the notebook a few minutes later, she lets out a satisfied sigh.

"What was that about?" I ask.

"Oh, I..." She clutches the notebook to her chest as her eyes dart from me to the others and back again. "I'm not sure I should say. We've been having such a nice time, and I've quite enjoyed having no one roll their eyes at me all morning."

I swallow a laugh. She and Jasper are as much two peas in a pod as Evan and Hadley are. "Go ahead. Tell us."

Lina takes a deep breath. "You know how I was stuck on my next book? I realized part of the reason was because it was missing something, yet I couldn't figure out what. Being here with the three of you gave me an epiphany. What the story was missing was *heart*. Family. It hit me that my main character should have sisters. Their relationship is messy sometimes and they fight and get irritated with each other, but ultimately they'd do anything for one another."

Silence hangs in the room, giving me déjà vu to when Hadley came out to the family yesterday. Was that really only yesterday? Time seems to work differently around the Perrys.

Hadley gives a quiet sniffle and clears her throat. "Well. Sounds like another best-selling, award-winning novel, Lina."

Sherée and I giggle at that, and even Lina chuckles softly. "I know you're teasing me, but I can't help hoping you're right."

By the time the last batch of cookies comes out of the oven, Jasper is hovering around the kitchen doorway. We finish tidying up and the other three girls traipse out of the kitchen while I hang back.

Jasper hurries into the room, looking relieved. He pauses when he sees me, and I realize he changed his shirt at some point between breakfast and now. I laugh delightedly as I take in the dark-green pullover sweater with the red-nosed reindeer on the front.

"Nice one, Mr. Darcy," I say.

Jasper's brow furrows. "It's...Perry."

I press my lips together to hold back the laugh-sigh combo that threatens to escape. "I meant Mark Darcy from the movie *Bridget Jones's Diary*. He wears a sweater just like that."

"Oh. I've never seen that movie, I just thought the sweater was festive. Do you think it's too much?"

It dawns on me suddenly that it's more than just the sweater that reminds me of Mark Darcy. Like Mr. Darcy, Jasper is kind of stuck up, very precise and proper, often rigid. Maybe watching *Bridget Jones's Diary* would help him get in touch with his softer side the way swoony Colin Firth's character does. "It's perfect," I tell him. "And you really should see the movie. It's one of Hadley's favorites, so I'm sure she'd be happy to watch it with you sometime in the next few days."

"I'll mention it to her." He gives me a stiff smile as he opens the pantry door and pulls out the Christmas apron I saw in there earlier. When he dons it, the image is almost too much for me; I simultaneously want to laugh, hug him and take his picture.

"Can I help you with dinner?" I ask. "I'm not the world greatest cook, but I'm decent at prep stuff."

"I appreciate the offer, Gwen, but I think I work best alone. You'd have more fun with the others anyway. My brothers were pulling out the board games last I checked."

"Oh. Okay." I trudge out of the kitchen. Someone should really talk to that man about how dismissive he is. I know he doesn't mean to be and I shouldn't take it personally, but it stings. Especially since I thought we made progress last night.

I pause abruptly, drawing Evan's attention. He shoots me a quizzical look and I hold up a finger, spinning on my heel and marching back into the kitchen. "Jasper?"

"Mm?" He has his hand elbow-deep inside the turkey. *Blech.* That right there is one of the many reasons I've never attempted to cook a turkey.

"Do you really work better on your own or are you just used to doing things on your own because nobody wants to help?"

He straightens and pulls something from inside the turkey, blocking my view so I can't see. Maybe he's more intuitive than I thought. When he's finished, he turns on the tap, glancing at me as he scrubs his hands with soap. "The latter, I suppose."

"So you're not necessarily *opposed* to someone helping you? Someone who might actually *want* to help?"

"No..." he says slowly, drying his hands on the nutcracker print towel hanging on the oven door.

"Well then, Jasper, I'm helping you make Christmas dinner. Where should I start? And do you have a spare apron?"

He stares at me with large, unblinking eyes. When his face finally softens and he gives me the first real smile I've ever seen from him, it's a thing of beauty. I feel like the Grinch must have when his heart grew three sizes on Christmas Day. If the lingering smile on Jasper's face is any indication, I think he feels it too.

❄ ❄ ❄

"There," Jasper says, clapping his hands. "All that's left to do is finish the gravy when the turkey comes out." He glances at his watch, then shucks his apron and drapes it over one of the stools at the kitchen island. "We have just enough time to take the Perry family photo before dinner. We should do it now while the light is still good."

He bustles from the kitchen, leaving me to remove my own apron—he *did* have an extra, packed away in his suitcase as a spare—before following him out. In the living room, he's directing his siblings toward the tree and telling them where to stand.

Evan breaks away from the others and comes over to wrap his arms around me. "Mmm, you smell like sage and cinnamon and a whole bunch of other tasty things. Good enough to eat." He nibbles at my neck and I let out a squeal.

"Get a room," Malcolm calls.

Evan raises his head and meets my eyes, his gleaming with a mixture of disbelief and amusement. "He did *not* just say that."

"Maybe we should start making out right here and give them a taste of their own medicine."

"I like the way you think." He dips down to kiss me, but we're interrupted by Jasper saying he'll be right back with his camera and he expects everyone to be in place when he returns. Evan releases me with a murmured promise to pick up where we left off later.

Jasper zips back into the room carrying a fancy camera and a black bag tucked under one arm.

"I can take the picture if you want," I offer.

"No need, I've got a tripod and a remote," Jasper says absently, getting everything set up.

"Okay. I'll just go check on dinner then, make sure everything's all right in there."

I'm halfway to the kitchen when Jasper calls my name. He rushes over, surprising me by planting his hands firmly on my shoulders. "I don't need you to take the picture because I want you to be *in* it. It's a family photo, Gwen."

"Oh. *Oh.*" His words sink in, leaving my eyes burning and my throat tight. "Okay. If you're sure."

"Of course I'm sure." He glances over his shoulder at the others. Most of them are still talking and laughing as they get into position, but Evan is watching us, brows drawn in concern. I signal to him to wait and turn my attention back to Jasper as he continues speaking.

"Remember how last night I said I'm only now starting to process my grief, even though my parents have been gone for years? I was thinking I'd look into seeing a counselor in the new year."

"I think that's a great idea, Jasper. I saw a therapist for a couple of years after my dad died and it really helped."

"I'm glad to hear that. Perhaps I'll even find someone who can teach me how to *not* be so utterly clueless when it comes to interacting with people. I often seem to do damage where none was intended." He squeezes my shoulders and tilts his head, giving me a self-deprecating smile that draws a teary laugh from me.

"Keep me posted on how that goes."

We join the others in front of the tree and Jasper clicks away at his handheld remote over and over until we're all groaning and laughing and begging him to stop so we can eat. Finally, Jasper leads the way into the kitchen, leaving the tripod and camera set up. I grasp Evan's hand, holding him back so I can peer at the last photo taken. We're all laughing, even Jasper. The tree looks magazine worthy, even with the tacky tinsel, and falling snow is visible through the big window behind the tree.

"I know Jasper would never go for it, but I think this should be the family photo for next year's Christmas card," I tell Evan.

He wraps his arms around my waist from behind and rests his chin on my shoulder. "It *is* pretty perfect. I think you're his new favorite, so I'm sure you could convince him."

I turn in his arms and loop my own around his neck. "I *am* pretty persuasive. And just for the record, in case it wasn't clear, you're *my* favorite Perry."

He pulls me closer and presses his lips to mine. "And you're *my* favorite soon-to-be Perry. Now and always. Merry Christmas, Gwen. Thank you for loving me, nutty family and all."

"Now and always," I promise, kissing him hard and pouring all of my love into it, hoping he feels every ounce of it. "Merry Christmas, Evan."

EPILOGUE

❄

Evan hands me a red envelope. A jolly-looking Santa twinkles up at me from the postage stamp in one corner, and the return address in the opposite corner bears Jasper's name.

"Is this what I think it is?" I ask, slicing into the envelope.

"The yearly Perry newsletter that Jasper writes and none of us have any say in? Yes, yes, it is. Pull out the letter first and leave the card for last."

"Bossy," I murmur.

We had as much say in the picture as we had in the newsletter: none. Jasper has come a long way in the last year, but he still likes to be in control whenever possible. Evan's reminder to pick my battles is never far where his oldest brother is concerned.

Evan pours us each a glass of wine and brings it to the kitchen table where I'm sitting. "Read it out loud," he says, sliding into the chair across from me.

I laugh, then realize he's serious. "You're so weird sometimes. Okay, here goes:

Dear family and friends,

So much has happened in the Perry clan in the last year!

Our family has grown this year in more ways than one. We were all thrilled to welcome a new generation of Perrys with the birth of Malcolm and Sherée's baby, Elizabeth, in September. We're all very excited to have a baby around at Christmas this year, and we can't wait to introduce Elizabeth to our many family traditions.

While Malcolm and Sherée were our newlyweds last year, this year that title has been passed to Evan and his lovely wife, Gwen. The pair wed in October in a beautiful autumn-themed wedding in Bellevue among a small crowd of family and friends. They spent two weeks honeymooning in luxury in the United Kingdom and came back with many wonderful stories and photos to share.

Lina—or as she's known to the public, Laurelina Peregrine—continues to experience great success in her writing career. Her second novel, More Than Yesterday, *was published recently and has already been optioned by a film studio. She's hard at work on her third novel.*

Hadley has found her calling working for a small local travel agency and planning people's dream trips. She's taken a few dream trips of her own, returning as frequently as possible to her favorite spots in Europe. Because she's often gone for weeks at a time, she moved out of her apartment and chose to make her part-time home with Jasper. The two never thought they would live together again, but are enjoying cohabitation immensely.

Jasper has embraced his role as uncle to baby Elizabeth and spends as much time with his niece as possible. When he's not doting on Lizzie, spending time around the city with Hadley, or working at the bank, he's busy helping Hadley plan the first ever Perry family vacation, scheduled for next summer.

Wishing you all a very Merry Christmas from our family to yours."

Evan tilts his head back and forth. "Pretty good. A lot less pretentious than every other year. I still can't believe he talked us into a family vacation, though." He shudders dramatically. "I'm beginning to miss the days of us only seeing each other at Christmas."

"Come on, you don't mean that."

"You're right, I don't." Evan's relationship with his siblings has come a long way since last Christmas. He alternately gives me credit and blame, depending on how things are going with them. They spent a lot of time in Bellevue with us preparing for our wedding, and we've visited them in Toronto often. Evan has even been to a few counseling sessions with Jasper, which seem to have benefited both of them.

He takes the newsletter from me and scans it with a small smile. "I'm surprised Lina didn't insist Jasper include *More Than Yesterday* in the list of new family members."

I nearly choke on my wine. "Well, *I'm* surprised he didn't mention the certain someone he's been seeing recently."

Evan gives me a lopsided smile, shaking his head. "Okay, Miss Matchmaker. It's early days yet, he probably didn't want to jinx it. Besides, he likely wrote this weeks ago, you know how he is."

"True. And that's *Mrs.* Matchmaker to you." I lean across the table to plant a kiss on his lips. "Should we see if Lina had Mitzy photoshopped into the family picture?"

Chuckling, Evan motions for me to take the photo card from the envelope. Despite it being a lovely picture of all of us, I can't help the disappointment that whispers through my mind.

"Turn it over," Evan says.

I flip the card over and let out a choked laugh. It's double sided, with the picture of all of us laughing on the back. Evan and I have that photo, along with a group wedding picture, and a shot of the two of us in Scotland during our honeymoon on the dresser in our bedroom.

Evan takes my hand and kisses the back. "Are you ready for another very Perry Christmas in a few weeks, Mrs. Perry? With the added chaos of a baby in the mix?"

"Bring it on, Mr. Perry."

* * *

Dear reader,

Thank you for taking the time to read *A Very Perry Christmas*. I hope you enjoyed Gwen and Evan's story. If you did, I'd love to hear from you! You can find all my contact information on my website - www.marielandryauthor.com.

I'd be incredibly grateful if you would take a few minutes to write a review of *A Very Perry Christmas* on your blog, GoodReads, and/or the ebook retailers of your choice. It doesn't have to be long—even just a few words describing your feelings. Reviews are so important because they help people decide whether to read a book or not. You have the power to influence other readers!

Thank you for your support. Every time I hear from a reader who was touched by my work, it confirms that I made the right decision to follow my dreams and become an author.

Keep reading past the acknowledgments if you'd like to read a chapter from my standalone contemporary romance *Only You*, where you'll meet Gwen and Evan's friend Ivy before she met the love of *her* life, hot Scot Hugh MacKinnon.

With love and gratitude,
~Marie

ACKNOWLEDGMENTS

Mum, there's a reason all of my books are dedicated to you and it's because you're the most important person in my life and my very best friend. Thank you for your unconditional love and support.

Jaimie Admans, I could write another 30,000 words solely about what an amazing friend you are and how grateful I am to have you in my life. You're one of the few things keeping me sane (okay, relatively sane) during the roller coaster that is 2020. Thank you for your encouragement, love, and support, and thank you for cheering me on when I decided to write this book in such a short amount of time. I don't know what I'd do without you. All the dinos, mince pies, nutcrackers, and Oscar Isaac gifs for you. Well, okay, the Oscar gifs are really for me, but as we've both pointed out, there's an OI gif for every occasion, plus he's just so damn pretty.

Brenda St John Brown, I'm so grateful you're my friend. Your wisdom and wit, along with your willingness to help, never cease to amaze me. Thank you for always being there to listen, and thank you for not only beta reading this book, but helping me—as always—with the blurb.

Kaley Stewart, thank you for being such a great friend, and thank you for reading an early version of *A Very Perry Christmas*. I can't wait to hug you in person and buy you a beer someday in the hopefully-not-too-distant future. Jacquelyn Middleton, thank you for your friendship, support, and generosity. We both know how isolating this business can be, and I'm glad I found a kindred spirit in you. Our book shopping and cake date in Toronto can't come soon enough, but until then I'll continue to send hugs down the 401. Tammy Bramley, thank you for encouraging me to write this story when I mentioned I wanted to but thought it was complete madness to attempt it so late in the year. You didn't doubt me for a second, and that, paired with your regular check ins, kept me going. Thank you for being such a wonderful friend and cheerleader.

And finally, endless thanks goes to all the bookstagrammers, bloggers, and other book-loving people who put so much time, effort, and love into talking about and promoting books. I've said it before and I'll continue to say it: you're the unsung heroes of the publishing world. An extra special shout-out to my bookstagram family for all your love and support. I love our not-so-little community, and I'm so grateful for all the friends I've made there.

Only You by Marie Landry

When Ivy reluctantly takes a part-time job at Santa's Village, it's a means to an end. Doing this favor for her pain-in-the-neck roommate means Ivy can have her apartment to herself again much sooner. The last thing she expects is Hugh—the hot Scot who just happens to be her new boss—asking her out on a date. And then another. And another.

Something about Hugh makes Ivy want to let her guard down and open up, which would be perfect if he wasn't possibly returning to Scotland in a matter of weeks. But maybe that doesn't matter. Maybe Ivy can learn to live in the moment and have a little fun, even if it means setting herself up for heartache later.

Only You is a standalone contemporary romance about taking chances, unexpected friendships, and holding on to the things—and people—that matter most.

Turn the page for a peek at the first chapter!

CHAPTER ONE

One perk of your best friend also being your boss: she sees when you're stressed to the max and tells you to cut out of work a few hours early.

I hardly know what to do with myself as I push through the doors of the high-rise building where Quest Marketing Solutions is housed. Should I go shopping? Get my nails done? Head to the bookstore, aka heaven on earth? As tempting as browsing books is, the only *truly* appealing thing is a nice warm bath in an empty apartment. And if I want to do that, my window of opportunity is small.

Alone time has become a novelty in the last few months since I reluctantly took in a roommate. Celia is one of those 'cousins' who's not an actual relative; her parents are good friends with the aunt and uncle who raised me after my parents were killed in a car accident, and our families spent a lot of time together. Between a six-year age difference and Celia's general snarkiness, we never connected. That didn't stop me from agreeing to perform my family duty when my aunt informed me Celia was moving back to town after dropping out of college, and then not-so-subtly suggested I offer to rent her the spare room in my apartment. Fan Chen is not someone you say no to, even when she's living halfway across the world in China and I'm here in Canada.

I try to live my life with no regrets, but saying 'yes' to Aunt Fan that day and extending an invitation to Celia has caused nothing *but* regrets. Big ones. Endless ones. In the last four months, Celia has had three different jobs, all of which she's been fired from for various reasons, including being surly with customers and failing to perform the tasks required of her. When we're at home, she's constantly bitching about something, plus she eats my food even though she has her own. Some days I feel like I'm one snide remark away from wringing her neck.

Alone time is definitely the way to go right now. For my sanity and for everyone else's personal safety.

When I reach my car, I toss my purse in the passenger seat and blast the heater. It's only early November, but there's a nip in the air that makes me think Mother Nature has forgotten it's still technically autumn.

Something shiny catches my eye, and I bend to pick up a gum wrapper from the floor. Celia seems to think my car is a garbage receptacle. Our schedules don't often mesh (thank god), so she grudgingly takes the bus most of the time. Whenever I *do* give her a ride anywhere, she inevitably leaves a mess for me to clean up—coffee cups, gum and granola bar wrappers, and that memorable time she left a chocolate bar on the backseat in August and it melted into a sticky brown puddle. I discovered it after setting my reusable cloth grocery bags on top of it. The chocolate never did come out, and I refuse to carry around a bag that looks like it has a poop stain on it.

During the ten minute drive home, I make a plan. Celia should be home around seven, so I need to maximize every blessed moment of my alone time. First, I'm going to have a bath. I've been showering since the first week Celia moved in and informed me, lip curled in disgust, that having a bath was like stewing in your own filth. I've been hoarding the luxury strawberry-champagne bath bomb my best friend Bridget gave me ages ago, waiting for a Celia-free moment to finally use it. Next, I'll pour myself a glass of wine—because I've never been above day drinking—and then I'll soak in the tub until I'm all pruny and fruity smelling. After that, I'll squeeze in a bit of TV if I have time.

I pull into the parking lot of my apartment building and hurry up to the third floor, smiling to myself the whole way. My smile fades as I reach my door and hear the TV inside. I unlock the door and shove it open. There, on the couch, is Celia, wrapped in a fluffy blue housecoat—*my* housecoat, if I'm not mistaken—with the TV playing some crime show, and her bare feet elevated on the coffee table.

My dreams of a nice relaxing afternoon pop like the soap bubbles I won't be seeing any time soon. Holding back a groan, I close the door with more force than intended, causing Celia to jump and whip around.

"Jeeze, you scared me!" She clutches her chest dramatically.

"Why are you home so early?" I ask, dumping my purse unceremoniously on the floor. The excitement of leaving work and envisioning a few hours alone has drained from my body, leaving me feeling wilted.

A flash of guilt passes over Celia's features before she turns back to the TV. "Oh, you know, they let me leave early today. Why are *you* home so early?"

Ignoring her question, I say, "They fired you, didn't they?"

Her shoulders slump. Without looking at me, she reaches for the remote to mute the TV. "They started playing Christmas music today, Ivy."

I wait for her to elaborate. When she doesn't, I say, "Okay...and?"

Celia huffs out an annoyed breath. "It's practically the beginning of November! They were playing the same songs over and over. This woman in my line mentioned how she'd heard whatever song was on twice already since being in the store. So I said it was *way* too early for them to be playing Christmas songs. As she was nodding along, all agreeable, I *might* have mentioned something about how Christmas isn't a real holiday anyway because Christians stole Yule from the Pagans and turned it into a Christian holiday, and most modern-day Christmas traditions are actually Pagan ones in disguise." She says all of this quickly until her last few words are running together and she's out of breath.

"*Celia.*" I groan, letting my head fall back against the front door. "You didn't."

"The woman seemed to think it was funny!" Her voice pitches higher with each word. "She was nodding and laughing, and then I guess the bitch went and reported me to the manager afterward."

I let the 'bitch' comment slide; I'm a big believer in choosing your battles, and I have more important things to consider right now. "Didn't we talk about how you can't say things like that to people? I warned you and the store warned you when they saw your previous employment record. They were willing to give you a chance and you blew it two weeks in! Nobody will want to hire you now. You know that, right?"

Despite still sitting with her back to me, I imagine she's doing one of her patented eye rolls. "Well, whatever. Maybe I'll just be a lady of leisure."

"And live off what? How are you going to pay rent and bills without a job? And buy food?" I stop myself just short of saying 'And save up enough money to get a place of your own?' This arrangement of ours is supposed to be temporary. Celia's parents thought I'd be a good influence on the wayward twenty-three-year-old and could help get her life together. They refused to let her move back home, and she couldn't afford to live on her own, which is why she's currently residing in my spare room and casting a pall over my entire life.

"I've got a bit of money saved for bills and stuff. And besides, you can afford this place without my share of the rent. You've been living here on your own for years."

My blood pressure spikes. I can *feel* the blood surging through my veins. My vision blurs, and for a moment I wonder if it's possible for a person's head to actually explode. "No," I say through clenched teeth. "Absolutely not. I'm not going to be some kind of sugar mama while you laze around all day. Not happening. You moved to town to work and save money so you could either go back to school or find a job you can stick with, and that's what you're going to do."

A bead of sweat rolls down my temple, and only now do I realize I'm still wearing my coat, scarf, and boots. I shuck them all and snatch my purse from the floor. "I'm going to take a bath," I announce, striding as fast as my short legs will carry me toward the bathroom.

"Ivy," Celia calls.

"I don't want to hear it, Celia! I don't know how dirty you think I must be, but a bath is not 'stewing in your own filth' if you bathe regularly like I do." I slam the bathroom door and sit on the toilet lid, dropping my head into my hands. "Deep breaths," I murmur to myself, massaging my temples and sucking in air like my life depends on it.

Shoving my hands into my hair, I start removing the pins from my updo. Celia and I look enough alike it's easy to believe we *could* be related. We have the same shade of almost-black hair, although mine has a bit of wave to it while hers is stick-straight. We also have similar brown eyes and were blessed with a clear complexion. But where Celia is easily identified as Chinese-Canadian, my mother's Caucasian genes dominated my dad's Asian roots. I've been referred to as 'exotic' and asked what country I come from more times than I can count.

I open the cabinet under the sink and pull out the toiletry bag where I keep my more expensive items, like my special occasion makeup, scented oils, and a few other things. Things like my bath bomb, which is now missing from where it was nestled between my glittery eye shadow and my manicure set. As I'm reaching for the medicine cabinet to see if it somehow ended up in there, my gaze catches the reflection of the bathtub in the mirror over the sink. The curtain is askew, and the tub has a pink ring

around it. Pink, like the very expensive, have-been-saving-it-forever bath bomb that's no longer where it should be.
"Celia!"

❄ ❄ ❄

**Want to read more? *Only You* is available now!
Visit www.marielandryauthor.com for details**

ABOUT THE AUTHOR

Marie Landry's life revolves around books; when she's not writing them, she's reading them, taking pictures of them for bookstagram, or blogging about them. An avid reader from a young age, she loves getting lost in characters' worlds, whether they're of her own making or someone else's. She particularly loves coming-of-age stories with as much of an emphasis on self-discovery as on romance...but don't leave out the romance!

She lives in a cozy apartment in Ontario, Canada with the best roommate ever, and can be found working in a room surrounded by Funko Pops and—you guessed it—books. When not doing bookish things, you can often find her cooking, exploring areas both familiar and new, watching TV, or taking photos. Her fangirl heart perks up at the mention of *Star Wars, Sherlock,* and *Doctor Who,* and you'll often find nerdy references woven into her books.

Marie loves to chat, especially with fellow book lovers. Here's where you can find her:

Blog: www.ramblingsofadaydreamer.com
Instagram: @sweetmarie_83 (bookstagram) or @rambling_daydreamer (author/personal account)
Twitter: @sweetmarie83
Facebook: Marie Landry, Author

❄ ❄ ❄

Printed in Great Britain
by Amazon